A Very Corporate Affair

Book One

D A Latham

ISBN-10: 1490309772
ISBN-13: 978-1490309774

DEDICATION

To my dearest, darling Allan

ACKNOWLEDGMENTS

With thanks to all my advisors

Thomas Darlington

Andrea Mills

Michael Harte

Rebecca Elliott

Johanna Ballard

Penny Harrison

Gail Hayward

And

Sam Yazdani

CONTENTS

CHAPTER 1

I stood on Welling station shivering in the cold, and trying to calm the butterflies fluttering around in my stomach. Today was the day of judgement at work. The day I would find out if my training contract would turn into a fully fledged job at Pearson and Hardwick, one of the big four law firms in London. If today went well, I would become a qualified, and gainfully employed, corporate lawyer. If today went badly, then six years of studying would be down the drain.

It had been a real slog to get this far. I came from a working class family, who didn't believe in social mobility, and thought I was wasting my time. I had worked hard at Bexley Grammar to get top grades and secure a place at Cambridge to study law and business. I had kept my head down through university and had put in enough effort to gain a first. A year long legal practitioner course led to my traineeship, and another two years of intense concentration at Pearson and Hardwick had followed, as I threw myself into the opportunity they had given me.

I looked around the grey, featureless platform. At six thirty in the morning, only the early bird commuters were present. Pale, pasty looking men in badly fitting suits looked resigned to another miserable day in mundane jobs. There was not one exciting or interesting looking person there. Suburbia doesn't really breed the people who make you sit up and take notice, I thought to myself. All the more reason to escape as quickly as possible.

A Very Corporate Affair

I'd enjoyed Cambridge as it had been a huge relief to be around intelligent, informed people who had been passionate about academia. My mum had never understood a thirst for knowledge, and had tried to get me to lower my aspirations and take a 'nice shop job' at sixteen. The thought of returning home tonight unemployed and a failure, confirming all her warnings about 'getting ideas above my station', made the butterflies ten times worse.

I arrived at the offices at quarter past seven, pausing in the stunning wood panelled lobby of the ancient law firm, and wondered if it would be the last time I would walk through on my way to work. I ducked into the cloakroom to change into my heels and shed my coat.

"Good morning Elle," said Roger, the security man who was based in the lobby, as I waited for the lift up to my floor.

"Morning Roger, today's the day."

"I wish you the best of luck. I'm sure you'll be fine, the time you get here everyday must have shown them how conscientious you are."

"Thanks. Hope so." I smoothed the front of my neat pencil skirt, and gripped my handbag a little tighter.

Once I had reached my floor, I made my way straight to my desk to switch on my computer, check my emails, and just wait. All the cases I had been assigned to work on had been completed, and as my traineeship had been near its end, they hadn't given me any new ones. For the last week or so, I had just been assisting the other trainees with their cases, doing their drudge work, and helping out in the filing room. I had felt that the lack of new cases being put my way was a bad omen, and if they were keeping me, they wouldn't have worried about giving me fresh work.

Checking my emails, I saw one from Mr Lambert, my line manager. I opened it.

From: Adam Lambert
To: Elle Reynolds
Subject: Interview
28th March 2013

Dear Ms Reynolds,

Your interview today will be held at 11am in room 7 on the 4th floor. In attendance will be Ms Pearson, Mr Jones, and myself.

Kind Regards
Adam Lambert

I stared at the email for a minute or two. It wasn't giving anything away. I decided I need a cup of tea. In the small kitchenette area, I realised that my hands were shaking as I filled the kettle. I needed to get a grip. The last thing I wanted to do was show nerves or weakness when the rest of my workmates arrived. Cool, calm and collected was the image I wanted to project at work, not needy, insecure or scared, no matter how I felt inside.

As the other trainees filed in, I could see how rattled they were. It was interview time for all of us who began in 2011, and usually only a quarter of the intake would be offered permanent jobs. Scanning the faces, I tried to figure out who had screwed up, who had excelled, and who would be a tough call.

"Why are you looking so pensive?" Lucy demanded, standing in front of my desk, "we all know you'll be ok, miss perfect," she teased.

"I don't know about that, they could easily decide I'm not posh enough to fit in," I said, fully aware of my lack of private schooling and accompanying posh accent.

"Don't be daft, the fact that you have a perfect record and are a bloody genius will easily outweigh the problem of a glottal stop." She smiled to let me know she was teasing.

"Wha times yuh mee-ing?" I said, in full south London accent, taking the piss.

"11.30. You?"

"11. Good luck."

"You too. If its good news, I'll treat us both to lunch in Bennies." Lucy came from a wealthy background and didn't have to watch the pennies as I did. She sauntered off, seemingly unconcerned about her fate being decided upstairs.

At ten to eleven, I rinsed my hands in cold water to avoid a sweaty handshake, and made my way up to the floor above. The secretary directed me to take a seat just outside the meeting room to await my turn. The door swung open, and a fellow trainee, John Peterson, came out looking as white as a sheet. I caught his eye, and he gave an almost imperceptible shake of his head. He had been one of the 'sure things' I had judged earlier that morning. My stomach sank into my boots.

"Miss Reynolds, you may go in now," said the secretary. I plastered on my best fake smile and entered the room. The three interviewers sat behind a long table, with a single chair placed in front of them. Mr Lambert smiled at me, and asked me to take a seat. I shook their hands, and sat down.

"Good morning Miss Reynolds, I'm sure you must be nervous, so I won't waste time on pleasantries," began Ms Pearson. My heart sank. "You have the highest work output rate of your year group, the best attendance and punctuality rate, and the best report from your superiors." My heart hammered, and I tried to stop myself blushing at her compliment. Ms Pearson was a managing partner, so remaining in control in front of her was extremely important.

"So I'm delighted to be able to offer you a permanent position at Pearson and Hardwick. Now your report states that you would like to specialise in corporate law, is that correct?"

I pulled myself together quickly enough to answer her, "yes, that's correct."

"Good. We have an opening in our corporate department at Canary Wharf. You can begin there on Monday. For the rest of this week you will be on paid leave, as Mr Lambert has indicated that you have taken no holiday at all this year. The salary will be eighty thousand per year, plus the grade 3 benefit package. Do you have any questions?" Ms Pearson looked at me intently.

"No questions, and thank you Ms Pearson, I won't let you down," I said, barely able to take it all in.

"I'm sure you won't. Now, please head over to HR, where they have your new contract ready for you to sign, and sort out your package, then I suggest you have some rest until Monday."

I smiled widely at the panel, "thank you for this opportunity," I said before heading out.

Over at HR I signed my new contract, collected the details of my new workplace, and perused the list of benefits I could choose as part of my package. As I didn't have a car to be subsidised, I chose gym membership, private health care and an enhanced pension. The HR lady assured me that the gym at the Canary Wharf building was superb, and useful for showering and changing facilities if I needed them. On my way back to my floor, I bumped into Lucy, who was sporting a wide grin

"Great news Elle, I got family law, just as I wanted. What about you?"

"Good news for me too, I got corporate, so Canary Wharf here I come," I replied with an equally big smile.

"Wow! They are the most prestigious offices in the firm, you must have done really well. I'll come and visit you there. Now, shall we meet by your old cubicle as I have to see HR before we go to lunch?"

"Great, see you in a bit."

I went back to my cubicle with my shoulders back, and a lightness I had never felt before. Success felt fantastic, and for the first time ever I could escape my background.

Bennies was a bistro type bar tucked away down one of the tiny passages that characterised the city. Lucy ordered a bottle of Moët while we waited for our overpriced sandwiches. We clinked glasses and gossiped about who got kicked out and who was kept on. It turned out that out of a hundred who began the training contract with us, only fifteen had been offered full contracts.

"So, what's your next plan? Are you moving nearer work?" Lucy asked.

"Sure am, I have the rest of the week off, so it's a good opportunity to look for a flat share or a studio. Mum's boyfriend wants to move in, and it's too small a flat to have all three of us there, so it's time to move out." I hugged myself with glee. Escape from the moaning about my getting up early, use of hot water and aversion to junk food.

Lucy broke my reverie, "my brothers friend is looking for a flatmate, he lives near Canada square. Would you like me to call him?"

"Oh yes please, that would be great." She pulled her phone out of her bag and prodded the screen.

"Hi James, it's Lucy Elliott. Have you still got that room available? Only one of my friends is looking for a flat near Canary Wharf." She listened to the other person, injecting a 'mmm' every now and then. "Yes it's a she, and she is a nice, hardworking, quiet, corporate lawyer. Yes I work with her.....yes.....no......ok I'll send her along this afternoon. Text me the address yeah." Lucy ended the call.

"Rooms still available then?" I asked.

"Yep. He's a bit fussy about who he shares with. James is a nice guy, and likes a quiet life. He works from home, so needs a flat mate who goes out to work, and isn't too noisy." Lucy's phone chirped as a text arrived with the address, which she forwarded to me.

A couple of other trainees from our year arrived to celebrate with us, nicking our champagne, much to my relief. I didn't want to view a flat half cut.

After lunch, I headed over to the docklands, taking the DLR. I had to double check the address, as the building looked way too swanky to be a flat share type of place. Pressing the buzzer, a voice came through, "who is it?"

"Elle Reynolds, Lucy sent me."

"I'll buzz you in. Take the lift to the fourteenth floor. My door is right in front of you." The buzzer sounded, and I pushed my way into a marble and glass lobby. I took in the silence, the deep carpet, and sense of restrained opulence. The lift was large, mirrored and silently sped straight up to floor fourteen, which I noticed, was the highest floor.

The door in front of the lift was open, and what could only be described as a bear was standing in the doorway. It was hard to gauge his age with all the facial hair, but I took a guess at early thirties. He was tall and broad, dressed in jeans and an old tshirt which showed off muscular, hairy arms. Through all the long, curly hair and copious beard, a pair of twinkly blue eyes reflected a smile. "You must be James? I'm Elle," I said, extending my hand out to him. He shook it warmly and invited me in.

"Did you find it alright?" he enquired, "and would you like a coffee?"

"Yes it was easy to get here, and yes I'd love a coffee if you're having one." He showed me through to what could only be described as a state of the art kitchen. James pulled two cups out of a cupboard and pulled two pods out of a drawer.

"What sort of coffee? I can do americano, espresso, latte or cappuccino."

"A latte would be lovely," I said, awed that there was a choice. If my mum remembered to buy fresh milk it was an event, and yet this hairy, bearded, bear-person had fresh coffee and fresh milk. I was impressed.

I found out that James was an app developer, and had built a few hit apps, which had enabled him to buy the apartment. He was working on a new app, and worked from home, so needed some peace during the day. I told him all about my promotion, and we toasted my success with fresh coffee, which made me giggle. He explained that Canada Square was quite literally round the corner, and my walk to work would be around five minutes.

"So why do you want a flat mate?" I asked.

He squirmed slightly, "I work from home, and sometimes barely speak to a living soul from one day to the next. I guess I get a bit lonely here on my own." He looked a bit sad.

"No girlfriend?" I wanted to make sure there was nobody to get jealous that a woman was moving in. The last thing I wanted was to put anyone's nose out of joint.

"Nope. My last girlfriend went to live in Australia, so don't worry, nobody to get arsey about a girl living here. I have to ask, any boyfriend?"

"No. I've been working like a demon for the last few years. No time for a man." Much to my mothers disgust, I thought.

"Well, I have no issue with you bringing friends back, but I'd rather not have a man move in here, so if you get serious with anyone, please bear that in mind."

"Will do. Can I see the room?"

"Sure, this way." James led me down a short corridor and opened a door. The room was enormous, with floor to ceiling windows covering one wall. There was just a large bed and a cabinet with a TV in the room. It looked a bit sparse. I walked over to the windows and stared at the view of the Thames.

"There's a dressing room through here, and an ensuite through that door," said James, pointing at two doors. Looking in the first one, I found a beautifully fitted out walk in wardrobe, with acres of hanging space, shoe racks and a dressing table. My paltry clothing collection would take up about a tenth of the space.

The ensuite was lovely. It had a large, deep bath, a separate shower, and a heated towel rail. It all looked brand new and pristine.

"How much is the rent?" I asked, suddenly nervous that I wouldn't be able to afford to live in this luxury.

"A thousand a month, but that includes all bills. Does that suit?" I breathed a sigh of relief.

"Fantastic, it's a deal." We shook hands. I arranged to pay the deposit and first months rent into James bank account via my laptop, and he gave me a key.

We bonded over another cup of coffee. I really warmed to James. He was just the right mixture of intelligence, geekiness and humour. We had thrashed out some basic house rules which, thankfully, didn't include hot water usage or rationing the gas. He also mentioned that he was an early riser, and hoped that it wouldn't be an issue for me to be quiet late at night. We both laughed when I pointed out that ten pm was staying up late for me.

I headed back to Welling with a spring in my step, eager to begin my new, London life. As predicted, my mum could barely contain her excitement at my moving out. She dug out the News Shopper and found an ad for a 'man with a van' who would be able to move all my belongings at short notice. He was able to do Thursday, so that left Wednesday to pack up, and get everything ready. I would still have a few days to unpack, settle in, and explore before starting work.

Mum was eager to help pack my belongings, and I actually didn't have much. The whole lot took us a morning to box and bag up. I had invested carefully in good work clothes, but apart from that, I didn't really buy a lot. Plus I had used the money I earned during my training contract to pay off my student loans, and build some savings, rather than blow it on clothes and makeup.

That afternoon, I decided to hop on a bus to Bluewater and treat myself to a haircut and some new work outfits ready for Monday.

I went into the swankiest salon there, and booked in for a trim. I kept my hair long, but the stylist added layers, and the whole effect was classy and grown up. Delighted with my new hair, I wandered round the boutiques trying on clothes until I found a fabulous navy dress and jacket combo which fitted like a dream, and projected just the image I was aiming for. I stocked up on tights and toiletries and bought a pair of navy heels to match my new dress. In a mad moment of optimism, I even bought a box of condoms before heading home.

The next morning a slightly grubby van pulled up outside the flat, and an even grubbier, skinny man got out. He wasted no time flinging my stuff in the back while I wrote out my new address for mum.

"You have fun, and don't work too hard," were her parting words of wisdom. No doubt Ray, her boyfriend was waiting round the corner for my van to pull away before rolling up with his bags.

As we pulled away from Welling, the excitement rose in my belly. This was the moment I had worked towards for six long years. My life could finally begin.

James helped van man with my bags and boxes, so with the three of us, it didn't take long. It took a further two hours to unpack and neatly hang my clothes in the closet.

"You don't have much stuff for a girl," said James, wandering in with two glasses of wine.

"I'm not a great shopper, and I've not had much spare cash to spend on clothes and stuff," I replied, a bit embarrassed by my meagre use of the dressing room. I aimed to spend 10% of my new salary on clothes every month to make sure I looked the part.

"Not criticising, just saying. I've got even less clothes than you," he said in a good natured way. He sat on the dressing table seat sipping his wine as I checked all my shoes for dirt before stowing them on the rack. He told me all about the new app he was working on, which sounded great, and described the other occupants of the building.

"The only unfriendly one is the fella on the floor below. Never says hello, and seems to bring lots of different women back. I saw one crying in the lobby once, said he threw her out. He's definitely one to stay away from."

"Thanks for warning me. He sounds delightful, not. Now is there a grocery store around here? I need to pick up a few bits."

"There's a small mart round the corner. What do you need?"

"Milk, bread, that kind of stuff."

"I had it all delivered today. There's loads in the fridge. I get everything ocado'd in. I have everything sorted for dinner tonight, thought you might be too busy with the move to worry about it."

"James, that's really kind of you, thank you. I'll pay you back."

"Nonsense, it's only a few groceries, and besides, I love to cook, but I never have anyone to cook for, so indulge me and let me prepare something." He smiled warmly, and wandered back to the kitchen area.

I hugged myself with glee. Sipping wine in a gorgeous apartment overlooking the river, with a new friend, and a new job. It was everything I'd imagined it would be.

"Elle," James yelled, "foods ready." I hurried into the kitchen as he dished up a pasta and tiger prawn concoction. He poured another two glasses of wine, and pushed one over to me.

"Bon appetite little Elle, and welcome to Canary Wharf. I hope you'll be very happy here." We clinked glasses.

"Thank you big James, and I'm sure I'm gonna love it." I took a bite of my pasta, it was all lemony and buttery, and delicious. "Wow, you are a great cook, this is gorgeous."

"You look like you need a bit of feeding up."

"I'm not a great eater. My mum only ever heated stuff up out of the freezer, so it was often better to go without than suffer the nightly unidentified breadcrumbed fare."

James laughed, a rich, deep, hearty laugh, "no wonder you're skinny. You need good, healthy, hearty food, especially with a pressurised job. Will they have you working all hours of the day and night?"

"Probably. I'm going in there as the lowest in the pecking order, so I'm in no doubt that I'll get the donkey work. Law is like that, hierarchy is everything. I'm pretty certain that I'll be given a cubby hole next to the bogs for my office, and the secretaries will be sly bitches. I don't mind though, I'm prepared to earn my stripes."

"I hated corporate life," James confided, "glad to be out of it. Hated sucking up to a useless wanker of a boss, and attending endless meetings. If I need a status meeting nowadays, I just look in a mirror."

"Do you always work alone? Or do you sometimes collaborate?" I asked.

"Always alone. I did one app a few years back with a designer, and it was a bit of a disaster, all style over substance, so since then, I do it all myself. So what made you go into law?"

I pondered his question. "Money really. Corporate law is a well paid profession, and I wanted to escape my background. I wanted to aim high, and I enjoy the intellectual rigour of law. I didn't want to be involved in criminal law because I hate grisly stuff, and family law is often emotionally draining. I like the detail of contract law, and the fact that its usually done in shiny, neat offices rather than police cells or prisons."

James smiled at me, "I admire your ambition, I wish I had more of it. I'm happy just sitting coding apps and dreaming up games."

"You did ok out of it," I said, sweeping my hand to indicate the apartment, "this place is fantastic."

"Yeah, I'm pretty lucky," he agreed.

I spent the first evening in my new home watching telly on the big flat screen in the living area. James had shown me how to use the coffee maker, and dishwasher, so I insisted he sat down while I cleared up after dinner, and made us both coffee. By nine, I was yawning, so bade him goodnight, and went to bed.

The next morning I was up at my normal time of half five. I wandered through to the kitchen to make tea, and discovered James boiling a kettle.

"Morning Elle, sleep well?"

"Morning, yeah great thanks. Is there enough water in the kettle for two?" James nodded. He looked even more dishevelled in his dressing gown and pyjamas, with his beard sticking out like bed hair. He pulled out another cup and threw a tea bag into it.

"So what's your agenda for today?"

"I'm gonna check out my new gym, pop into my new office to say hi, and explore my surroundings. Anything you need me to bring in?"

"Don't think so, I'll text you if I think of anything. I've got stuff in the fridge for dinner tonight, so don't worry about food."

"Ok, thanks, just let me know. I'm gonna take a shower now and head out." I took my tea back to my room and drank it while staring at the view from my window. After a luxurious shower, I dried my hair as I watched the stylist do, and applied a touch of makeup. I decided that trousers and flats were best bet for the day I had planned, so dressed in neat but trendy trousers and a simple cashmere jumper. As I wasn't sure what time the gym would open, I went back to the kitchen and made another tea. James wasn't around, so I sat quietly at the island and read through the bumf on the gym that HR had given me. It all looked pretty straightforward. I would have unlimited use of the facilities, and only pay for personal training. I checked the opening hours, finding that it opened at six. I would be able to do a workout in the mornings and still be at my desk by seven thirty, perfect. I finished my tea and placed mine and James cups in the dishwasher before heading down.

The lift stopped and the doors slid open while I was looking at my map of the area, and I automatically began to walk out, bumping straight into someone stepping in.

"I'm so sorry," I began, before noticing we were not in the lobby, and I had just bumped into Adonis himself. "I thought I was on the ground floor." I said lamely.

"Just be more careful," he snarled, before studiously ignoring me for the rest of the journey down. Must be the man James warned me about I thought. James didn't tell me he was sex on legs though. I surreptitiously studied him as he exited the lift. Short dark hair, bespoke suit, and a face that would be handsome if he smiled.

I was indeed five minutes away from the Canary Wharf tower, which rose majestically to top the surrounding skyscrapers. I followed the directions to the gym on the lower ground floor. It was a health enthusiasts dream, row upon row of state of the art equipment, complimentary towels, pristine changing rooms, and a full list of fitness classes. I booked in for an orientation session the following day, and picked up a class timetable. I exchanged my voucher from HR for my gym pass at the desk, and wandered around for half an hour, checking out the changing room and the machines.

My new office was based on the 34th floor of the tower, so at nine, I went up there to introduce myself. The receptionist was a pretty Asian girl, called Priti, who seemed efficient and welcoming. She introduced me to a few of the other lawyers, all of whom seemed friendly enough.

"I can show you where you'll be working," said a geeky, skinny man who introduced himself as Peter Dunn. "They told me you were starting Monday, so your desk is all ready."He showed me through a large open plan office full of people to a corridor of glass fronted offices. Pushing a door open, he revealed a large office with four desks. Two desks were occupied by men. Peter explained that he sat at the far end, and the final desk was earmarked for me. I introduced myself to the other two.

"I'm Adrian Jones, and he's Matt Barlow. So your the ex trainee we have to get up to speed then?"

"That's me. I hope you don't mind having a newbie around," I said, hoping to disarm them. I knew that nobody liked babysitting newbies.

"I'm sure we'll cope, and it'll be nice having a bit of eye candy around, eh boys? This firm has an ugly secretary only policy," Adrian sniggered.

"I'll do my very best to look pretty gentlemen, just don't forget I'm not a secretary." I smiled to make them think I was teasing.

"If you wear a tight blouse I promise I won't get you making tea," quipped Matt.

"I'll see what I can do," I laughed, "as long as you'll be able to concentrate on your work if I'm in here with my cleavage on show."

"She's gonna have every hotshot in the tower salivating over her, you have no chance," laughed Peter, looking amused at the adolescent behaviour of his colleagues. I had fully expected sexist banter, and it all seemed quite harmless. Certainly my office mates seemed friendly enough, and I was confident I'd be able to handle them.

I didn't hang around long, as I wanted to explore the whole area. I discovered the vast shopping complex beneath the tower, looking out for decent lunch places and a dry cleaners. I found wine bars, restaurants, and pubs for evenings out, and a gorgeous deli for supplying food for evenings in. I stopped off at a Starbucks for a coffee, and settled into a sofa to check my map.

"May I join you?" My head snapped up at the masculine voice. Adonis from the apartment block was standing in front of me.

"Sure," was all I could manage. I went back to my map. I could do rude too. He coughed slightly, which made me look up. He was staring intently.

"You just came out of Pearson and Hardwick," he said.

I stared back, "yes," I replied, giving nothing else away. He unnerved me, which I didn't like. I hoped he didn't work for them as well. He blew on his coffee before sipping it. I watched his mouth. He had the sexiest mouth.

"So what were you doing there?"

"I beg your pardon?" How rude was this man? Out of all the ways to frame a question, he had to pick the worst.

"Are you a secretary?" I almost spat my coffee at him

"No I'm most certainly not. It's none of your business why I was there." I watched as his eyes flashed. I couldn't work out if he was laughing at me or angry.

"I suppose it's not, I just saw you in their offices. I was in there signing a contract," he said.

"Are you a client?" I asked, suddenly wary of upsetting him.

"No, I was there with my own legal team, they had drawn up a contract for the other party. So are you going to tell me why you were there?"

"I start work there Monday, I'm a lawyer for Pearson and Hardwick, just moving over to corporate. Went there today to introduce myself."

"So are you going to introduce yourself to me? Seeing as you nearly knocked me over at home and work two floors below me in the tower?"

"I'm Elle Reynolds. I just moved into the apartment, James' new flatmate. Have you lived there long?"

"About two years. I'm Oscar Golding, and it's very nice to meet you Elle." He leaned forward and shook my hand. His hand was surprisingly warm and soft for such a harsh looking man. I wanted to get a smile from him to see if I was right about him being more handsome. I gave him my best beaming smile, hoping he would reciprocate. He just about managed to turn the corners of his mouth up when his phone rang. As soon as he saw the screen, he scowled and excused himself. I went back to my coffee and my map.

I picked up a box of Krispy Kremes before heading home. James came out of his study when he heard the front door.

"Thank god you're back. I was going boggle eyed at my screen in there. What you been up to?" He made coffee and set out the box of doughnuts while I told him about the gym, my office, and the shopping mall.

"I bumped into our downstairs neighbour this morning, quite literally. He really is a strange one. Snarled at me in the lift, saw me in Starbucks this afternoon and managed to piss me off again."

James laughed, "how did he manage to piss off a jolly little thing like you?"

"Said he saw me in the Pearson and Hardwick offices and asked if I was a secretary." James' eyebrows shot up.

"Why did he assume you were a secretary? Stupid man."

"Quite. He really is quite unpleasant. Never smiles either." I sipped my coffee, and smiled at James demolishing the pile of doughnuts. "I did make sure he wasn't a client though."

"Clever move. Never a good idea to make a client feel like an idiot." We both laughed.

James made fajitas that evening, which were delicious. Afterwards I had a long hot bath before putting my pyjamas on and joining him for a bit of telly and a glass of wine before I turned in.

16

Chapter 2

Friday evening, James invited me to join him and his friends for a drink in one of the local bars. I wore my one and only little black dress, and heels, slipping a leather coat on for the walk there. James actually scrubbed up quite well, much to my surprise, and introduced me to his group of friends. They were a mixed bunch, with two couples, two single men, and an older woman called Jenny, who said she was an artist. She had flame red hair, dressed in a flowing caftan and called everyone 'poppet'.

"Poppet, this girl is divine," she said to James, "is she hetero?" I blushed puce.

"Yes she is, so mitts off," he replied, before whispering in my ear, "she's a raging dyke, so don't go to the ladies with her."

Neither of the two single men there floated my boat, one being short and chubby, and the other so thin he was almost transparent. James introduced them as Tom and Gary, although I didn't really work out which was which. The two couples seemed nice, but appeared to be happier sitting in their coupley foursome chatting about Ikea, or whatever couples talk about. We all stood around drinking bottles of beer, and listening to Jenny's funny stories.

One of the Tom/Gary men sidled up and asked if I liked going to the cinema, before blushing almost purple.

"Not really my thing, I can never stay awake for a whole film," I replied, shutting down any prospect of him asking me for a date to the pictures. The last thing I wanted to do was turn one of James friends down, so I moved away and went to the bar to order more beers. Thankfully, he seemed to get the hint, and turned his attention to Jenny.

James and I were both swaying a bit as we walked back to the flat, giggling at Jenny's outrageous flirting with me. At one point I'd had to almost hide behind James as she openly stared at my chest.

"She's not normally that bad. She flirts a lot, but she really couldn't take her eyes off your chesticles tonight." James sniggered at the thought.

"I don't think my tits have ever been so gawped at. Even blokes lift their eyes to my face after a while."

"Never mind little Elle, take it as a compliment. At least you pulled." We both laughed.

I woke late the next morning, with a bit of a fuzzy head. I staggered into the kitchen to make tea. There was no sign of James, so I made tea and a couple of slices of toast. I was checking my emails when James appeared looking bleary eyed. He poured a cup of tea and sat opposite me at the island.

"Did you make me drink all that beer last night?"

"Nope. You did it all by yourself."

"Next time, can you remind me I get shocking hangovers please."

"Will do. Although I'm surprised a big fella like you can't hold his beer."

"Not as surprised as I am that a little shrimp like you can."

I went and got him some paracetamol from my bathroom cabinet, and made him an espresso to perk him up, before changing into my gym kit and heading off to my orientation session.

The gym was pretty empty due to it being a Saturday. My instructor, Lorna, showed me round all the machines before rating my fitness level and giving me a health check. I stayed behind to do a workout. I programmed my iPod to my running playlist, and hopped onto a treadmill. Starting with a brisk walking pace to warm up, I worked my way up to a fast paced run. I loved to run, finding it the ideal exercise to clear my head and help me think.

After half an hour, I slowed the treadmill, and stopped to take a swig of water. The gym had filled up a bit while I'd been in my own world, and I became aware of Oscar standing in the doorway staring at me. Determined not to be intimidated, I gave him a beaming smile and a little wave. He looked a bit disconcerted, and gave a half wave back before walking to the furthest running machine in the room, and starting his run.

I did another half hour on the weights machines, working my body methodically to gain maximum benefit. I liked being fit and strong, and took pride in having an athletic figure despite the hours I spent sitting at a desk.

Back in the changing room, I put on my swimsuit, and headed out to the pool area. I liked to finish a workout with a swim and a sauna. I decided on 25 lengths of front crawl, which didn't take too long, as I could swim pretty fast. The sauna at the end was to be my reward for a good workout. I pulled open the wooden door, only to find Oscar sitting on one of the benches. *Damn,* I thought, annoyed at bumping into him again when I just wanted to sit and sweat in peace.

"We must stop meeting like this Miss Reynolds," he said. I simply raised an eyebrow, and sat back on the bench, closing my eyes. He didn't take the hint.

"That was quite an impressive workout," he went on, not twigging that I was practically ignoring him. I opened one eye. He looked hot in just shorts. Nice smattering of chest hair too.

"Just a normal workout," I said quietly.

"How often do you work out?"

"Every day usually, if I can." I wanted him to go away, his half naked body in close proximity was having a bit of an effect on me, which I didn't like.

"Would you like to join me for a coffee or something when you finish in here?" I opened both eyes in surprise. A man who had never so much as smiled at me was asking me for coffee! He still looked miserable.

"Sorry, I have an appointment I need to get to." I really didn't want to spend time with this scowling bundle of anger issues, and I really wanted to get my nails done.

"Another time then," he said, as he stood up and walked out of the sauna. I breathed a sigh of relief. I stayed in there another five minutes, enjoying the peace, before heading into the showers.

Feeling squeaky clean, I wandered down to the shopping arcade to see if the nail bar could fit me in. Forty minutes later, I was perfectly manicured with long lasting gel polish in a sophisticated nude shade. I text James to see if we needed groceries, then headed home, stopping at the mart for milk.

Back home, I told James about my encounter with Oscar at the gym.

"Hmm, seems like he's set his cap at you. Just be careful, there's something about him that's just not quite right."

"I just don't understand how he thinks he can chat me up without cracking his face. It's a shame, he would be good looking if he smiled a bit. He's got a killer body though."

"Were you ogling him in the sauna, you naughty girl?"

"A bit. Couldn't really help it, he was only wearing shorts. I was looking, not ogling," I said primly, which made James laugh.

"So is he muscular? Hairy? Scrawny?" James asked, prompting me to guess he was gay.

"Decent muscles, little bit of chest hair, long legs."

"Is that your type?"

"I don't have a type," I said, which was true. All the boyfriends I'd had, had been wildly different. "What's your type?" I asked James.

"Blondes," he replied quickly.

"Male or female?" He looked amused at my question.

"Female. You didn't seriously think I was gay did you?"

"I wasn't sure," I said, a bit embarrassed. To be honest, James had come across a bit asexual, like I thought a brother would be.

"Not gay, just not one to chase women. I had a bad breakup last time, so I'm sworn off relationships."

"Oh. What happened?"

"I thought she was the one, so I proposed. She said no, and then buggered off to Oz with my best friend. I gather they're married now." From the little bit of James' face I could see, he looked sad.

"That's awful."

"Yeah, well......shall we watch a film? We have Netflix, so there's loads of choice. We scrolled through the film menu and settled on an action movie. I poured us each a glass of wine, and we sat in companionable silence.

The next day, I did my laundry, and headed over to the gym for the 11am yoga class, as I was a touch aching from the day before. Thankfully I didn't run into Oscar again. Back home, James had bought the Sunday papers, and was reading them at the kitchen island, pausing only to make coffee, and scoff the Danish pastries I'd bought.

Monday morning I was in the gym at six am, and did a precise forty five minute workout before showering. I did my hair, makeup, and got dressed, managing to walk into the office at seven thirty. I was surprised to see a few dozen people there already.

Peter was the only one in my personal office present. He was working at his computer when I walked in.

"Morning Elle, good weekend?"

"Great thanks. Yours ok? Any idea what I'm gonna be doing today?"

"Lewis Jones is your line manager. He's the one who assigns you your cases, and monitors your workload. He's in the office next door," Peter pointed to his left, "and he's in already."

I headed to the next office, and knocked on the door.

"Come in, you must be Elle Reynolds, I'm Lewis Jones, your manager.

"Pleased to meet you Mr Jones." I shook his hand. He was middle aged, rotund man, with sharp, intelligent eyes.

"Lewis, please. I'm going to start by showing you around the offices to orientate you with the facilities and the people who work here, then today you will be shadowing me to get a feel for the cases we're currently running. Sound ok?" He smiled warmly.

"Sounds great." I followed him out of his office to meet everyone.

The morning passed in a blur. Lewis was as sharp as a tack, and I knew I'd learn a lot from him. At midday, Priti came to find me to take me to lunch. She showed me a cute little cafe tucked in a corner of the arcade. We picked out our sandwiches and coffees, and grabbed a small table. I really liked Priti, she was bubbly, gregarious, and seemed to know everyone and everything. She pumped me for information, finding out that I didn't have a boyfriend, had just moved, and shared an apartment with a bear-man called James.

"There are loads of hot men working in the tower, you'll definitely find a boyfriend. There are a few super-hot ones too that everyone salivates over. The best one is a dreamboat Russian who's the CEO of a finance type company. He only goes out with supermodels though."

"Hmm. Is he a client of ours? I wouldn't ever date a client."

"No, he's been in when our clients have sold to him though. You should have seen the secretaries, they were practically dribbling." Priti smiled at the thought. By the time we headed back to work, we were firm friends.

The rest of the afternoon flew by. Apart from one of the secretaries, who had been a bit offhand, everyone seemed friendly and helpful. Lewis gave me a contract to look over, so I sat at my desk and went through it line by line. At five, Priti came into my office.

"You just had flowers delivered," she said without preamble. I hurried out to reception to find a large bouquet of lilies, which perfumed the entire area. Puzzled, I found the card nestled amongst the blooms, and ripped it open.

Hope your first day was successful
Best wishes
Oscar Golding

Priti watched me frown, "not expecting them?" She asked.

"From a man I met in the coffee shop last week. Not someone I'm terribly keen on. I just keep bumping into him." Priti took the card from me to read. Her eyes widened as she read it.

"Do you know who this is?"

I nodded, "he lives in my flats and works out in my gym. Never cracks his face though, gotta be the most miserable sod on the planet."

"You don't know who he is do you?"

"Not really."

"Chairman of Goldings bank, two floors up. I think his great grandfather set it up. He belongs in the super-hot club. Every woman in this tower is gonna be green with envy." I blinked at her. He had told me in Starbucks that he worked two floors up. I hadn't bothered to look up which company was on that level.

"Getting his PA to send me flowers isn't asking me out. He's just a neighbour being friendly, so don't waste your time greening up." I plonked the bouquet in the corner and went back to the contract.

James' eyebrows shot up when I walked in that evening lugging the bouquet as well as my gym bag and handbag. Before he could ask, I pulled the card out of my pocket and handed it to him.

"An admirer already? He seems to be pursuing you quite aggressively. I bet he won't let up. His type never do."

"Hmm, I'll handle him. Priti told me who he is. Some hotshot banker. If I keep ignoring him, he'll get the message eventually." I busied myself arranging the lilies in a vase James had pulled out, while he dished up some food.

"I made chicken chasseur tonight. Hope that's ok," he said.

"Great thanks, it smells delicious. I'm starving." I told James all about the rest of my day over dinner.

"So you're gonna hold out for the Russian financier?" James smirked.

"No. Apparently he only dates supermodels. I didn't work my way up to this job to find a boyfriend you know. I can manage perfectly well without a man on my arm, besides I haven't even seen that one yet, he might be pig ugly."

James laughed, "doubt it if all the secretaries knickers hit the floor when he walks through. Some people just have it all."

I changed the subject to James' day. He told me all about the new app he was coding which would allow people to pay each other via their mobiles. He hoped to sell it to either a bank or a large payment portal. He told me about the banks that had expressed interest already. Mobile phones weren't as susceptible to viruses, so were more secure than PC banking systems. I could see how animated he became when he discussed his work, he clearly enjoyed it more than he let on.

After a hot bath, I crashed into bed, exhausted. I reasoned that it had been a good first day, despite the interruption of the flowers. Within five minutes I was asleep.

I woke up at half one to the sound of faint piano music, a heartbreakingly sad melody. I padded through the apartment to see if it was James. His room was in darkness, as was the rest of the flat. Straining my ears, I worked out that it must be coming from downstairs. I padded back to bed, and lay listening for a while, until my eyes grew heavy, and I went back to sleep.

Next morning, I mentioned it to James. He said he'd never heard it before, but as his bedroom was the far side of the apartment, he wouldn't be directly above it.

"Must have been old misery guts upset that you didn't swoon at his feet over the flowers," said James, glancing over to the lilies. I rolled my eyes.

"Was I meant to knock on his door to say thanks do you think?" I asked.

"He probably would have bitten your head off if you had, so no, but I think he'll be hanging around you before the weeks out."

I tried to ignore the sense of foreboding and get myself ready for work.

Thankfully, the rest of the week proved uneventful, although busy. There was no further contact from Oscar, which I was pleased about. Lewis had been delighted with the work I'd done on the contracts he'd assigned me. I'd managed to spot a couple of errors and issues, which had earned me brownie points, and Lewis some high praise from a grateful client.

Friday afternoon, Lewis poked his head round my door, and asked me to join him for a contract negotiation. He explained that he would do the actual negotiating, but it would be a good opportunity for me to observe. I smoothed down the front of my dress, and followed him into one of the conference rooms. He explained that one of our clients was negotiating with a venture capitalist in a debt for equity deal.

Our clients arrived first, looking nervous. After introductions, we all sat and waited for the other party. We didn't have to wait long, they turned up exactly on time. A group of suited men walked into the room, before parting to reveal the most beautiful looking man I'd ever seen. He had piercing blue eyes, silky black hair that flopped slightly over his forehead, and the squarest jaw I'd ever seen outside of a cinema. His name was Ivan Porenski. *The Russian*, I thought, it had to be. I concentrated on appearing cool and collected while introduced to him, but felt the electricity as he shook my hand. We all took our seats, and the meeting began.

I was grateful that Lewis was doing the talking, as my brain kind of fried a bit around Ivan at first. He commanded the room, charisma pouring off him by the bucketload. His English was perfect, although heavily accented, and he led the negotiation. I could see he was losing our clients with the fiendishly complicated detail he was demanding, so I slipped a note to Lewis under the table to that effect. I didn't want to accuse Ivan of trying to bamboozle our clients, but it looked as though he was trying to do just that. The numbers he was spouting in a rapid fire simply didn't add up.

I slipped another note to Lewis. *Works out at 63% over the term, not 53%.* A note came back, *are you sure? I lost count.* I caught his eye and nodded.

"We will need some time to check these figures Mr Porenski, my colleague has indicated a possible discrepancy in the percentage figures you quoted," said Lewis. I prayed to god I was correct. The Russian pinned me with such a furious stare, I knew at that moment that I had indeed been right.

Lewis insisted on a break in the meeting to check the figures. During the recess, we calculated and checked. I had indeed been correct. I breathed a sigh of relief. When we reconvened, Lewis used the issue with the figures to negotiate a far better deal for our client than had previously been on offer. I could see that the Russian wasn't happy, but thankfully he acquiesced gracefully. I even caught him looking at me with an amused smile.

We ended the meeting and agreed to reconvene the following week to sign the revised contract. After both parties had left, Lewis gave me a pat on the back.

"Well done Elle, you just saved our client 10% of his company, quite an achievement doing those figures as quickly as you did. That Russian is quite a bag of tricks. Catches a lot of people on the back foot."

"I can understand why, he was bloody fast, and so confident, I almost didn't believe my own figures," I admitted, trying hard to loosen the tension in my shoulders.

"Monday morning, we'll revise the contract, in the meantime, have a great weekend. You've had a stellar first week." He smiled warmly before walking off to his office, loosening his tie as he went.

I wandered back to my office to shut down my computer, and grab my gym bag. The other three stopped work as soon as I walked in.

"Heard about your triumph against the Ruskie," said Adrian, with a touch of admiration in his voice.

"Good news travels fast here," I replied, unsure where this was going.

Matt looked at his watch, "around the tower in three, two, one. That's it, you're famous." They all sniggered.

"I doubt it very much." I said, collecting my gym bag, "anyway, I'm off, have a great weekend." I walked out through the main floor, convinced I could hear whispering. As I stepped into reception, I saw Oscar standing by the door. He stepped into my path.

"I need to talk to you," he said, his usual scowl in place.

"Oh? What about? Thanks for the flowers by the way, they were lovely," I replied, keeping my composure.

"Come with me, I'll tell you on the way." I followed him out, waving goodbye to a dumbstruck Priti on the way. Lugging my heavy gym bag, I struggled to keep up with him as he strode along the corridor to the arcade. The lift had been full, so he hadn't said a word all the way down.

"Will you slow down a bit," I said loudly. He turned and grabbed my bag off me and carried on at the same pace. I trailed after him into a wine bar. He led me to a secluded table, and dumped my bag on the floor.

"Drink?"

"White wine please." By now I was beyond curious. He went over to the bar and bought two glasses of wine. Setting them down on the table, he sat opposite me.

"So you got one over on Ivan?"

"How fast does news travel? In actual fact I just stopped Ivan getting one over our client, different thing. How do you know?"

"I'm his banker." Oscar smiled, "and not many people can keep up with him, he was impressed."

"Good. Did you know you look entirely different when you smile?" That made him laugh. He looked even better.

"Thank you for the compliment, but I wanted to let you know that I overheard him ordering a background check on you."

"I have nothing to hide, he can check as much as he likes."

"Just be careful around him. He has a reputation with women." I nearly spluttered into my wine.

"Pot, meet kettle. Anyway I'm a big girl thanks."

"What do you mean pot and kettle?" He looked affronted.

"Been warned about you too. I have sharp little ears you know." I watched him blush.

"What am I meant to have done?"

"I heard you were quite the playboy. Although I will admit its only hearsay, which is inadmissible as evidence."

"Hmm, don't believe everything you hear. Did you enjoy your first week?" He tried to change the subject.

"Yep, it was great. I love working in the tower, and my new flat is fantastic. By the way, you live in the flat below don't you? Was you playing piano music last night?" I watched his face carefully. He remained impassive.

"Yes, I tried to buy the one you're in, but your flatmate beat me to it. Did I disturb you last night?"

"Not really, I was awake and heard it, that's all. It wasn't loud. James sleeps on the other side of the apartment, so has never heard you." I was dying to ask why he was listening to maudlin music at one thirty in the morning, but decided against it. "Priti told me you work in a bank."

"That girl knows everyone's business. Yes I work for the family firm, which is as much a curse as a blessing." Oscar stared into his glass.

"In what way?" I pressed. He had me intrigued, and this softer, more human side was definitely proving quite attractive.

"It's a great job, great money and perks and all that, but I have to live up to expectations at all times, which can be difficult. I wouldn't give it up or anything like that, I just sometimes wish I didn't have to be Oscar Golding, bank chairman and upright citizen." I tried to look sympathetic, but struggled. He owned a bloody bank and was whining about it. He should spend a bit of time in a south London council flat if he wanted something to moan about.Instead, I kept schtum. He broke my musings by asking, "have you got plans this weekend? I'd love to take you out to dinner." He smiled hopefully, seemingly having learnt that I liked smiles.

"I could do tomorrow evening," I said, intrigued as to where he'd take me.

"Great, I'll pick you up at 7.30," he said, "wear a dress." With that he got up and pecked my cheek goodbye, before striding off.

I couldn't wait to get home to tell James about it.

Chapter 3

I sat at the kitchen island recounting my day to James. He listened intently without comment until I got to the part about going out to dinner with Oscar.

"Are you sure that's wise?"

"I can handle him, but if you hear screaming tomorrow night, come and rescue me."

"I won't be around. You're not the only one who had an eventful day. I'm off to the states in the morning. Apple called, they want to collaborate with the major banks in the development of mobile banking apps. Guess who they want to work on it?"

I squealed, "that's amazing news, congratulations. How long are you gonna be out there?"

"Only about a week this time. Silicon Valley and New York. It's a hard life eh?" James pulled a bottle of champagne out of his capacious fridge, and opened it with a flourish. He poured two glasses full, and raised his in a toast, "to a successful week."

"Cheers," I said, clinking his glass with mine, "and may next week be even better."

James left early the next morning to catch his flight. It was the first time I had actually been alone in the flat since moving in. I nosed around the spare bedroom, and peeked into James office. It was a stark room, with just a desk and a few bookshelves. I wondered how he spent so many hours every day in such a featureless room. I left the office and closed the door, deciding not to poke around or pry. James' bedroom was larger than mine, and had the same large windows and river view. There were no pictures, paintings, or other clues to the man who slept here. The room was tidy to the point of bare, giving it a sterile look that was at odds with James dishevelled appearance. My curiosity satisfied, I went back to the kitchen to make a latte, and plan what I was wearing that evening.

I looked around the arcade after my workout. I wanted something new to wear, so checked out the boutiques until I came across a pretty, and sophisticated wrap dress. I tried it on, and decided it was just the right mix of demure and sexy. It was important to me to look good that evening to cover up the insecurity I felt around people like Oscar. I also bought new lingerie and stockings, just in case.

Back home, I took my time getting ready, paying particular attention to my hair and makeup. By half seven, I was a bundle of nerves. I nearly jumped out of my skin when there was a knock at the door.

Oscar looked delicious. He was wearing a suit, bespoke by the look of it, with a deep blue shirt, and a deep blue tie. He smiled as I invited him in while I grabbed my coat and bag.

"You look lovely," he said, kissing my cheek. His close proximity was heady.

"Thank you, so do you. Where are we going tonight?"

"I didn't know what you'd like, so I chose The Ivy. Hope that's ok," he replied. *Good choice Oscar,* I thought.

"Great choice," I said, flashing my best, most dazzling smile. We travelled down to the ground floor in silence. A cab was waiting outside to drive us to the West End.

The Ivy was packed, and I wondered how he'd managed to get a table at such short notice. We perused the menu, and he said he liked the Devonshire chicken, which was for two people, if I wanted to share. When the waiter arrived, he ordered for both of us, and chose a bottle of Sancerre. Once he'd ordered, and the waiter disappeared, he stared at me, which was a touch disconcerting.

"So tell me about yourself Elle."

"You already know where I live and where I work. You know I like the gym, and there's not much more to tell. What about you? Where did you study?"

"Oxford. I went straight into the family firm afterwards to learn the ropes. Took over as chairman three years ago when my Father died."

"How old are you?"

"Thirty two. How old are you?"

"Twenty four. I did three years at Cambridge, a year legal practitioner, then straight into the law firm I'm with now. Did my traineeship, and got promoted." I left out the bit about coming from south London. Somehow, I felt I shouldn't share that with him. "That must have been hard, taking over a bank at twenty nine, plus dealing with losing your Dad." His scowl was back on his face, and I wondered if I'd said the wrong thing.

He shrugged, "it's what I was groomed for since birth, so it was just part of what was planned for me. Things are done.....differently in families like mine."

"Oh?" I raised my eyebrows, prompting him to go on.

"Well, you know, legacy and all that." *What was he on about?*

"So what else is expected of you?" I needed to find out more.

"Don't be coy, Elle. Your family probably expect the same from you." I gave him a quizzical look over my smoked salmon. "They expect me to marry and have children to carry on the family name, and the bank." He looked exasperated at having to spell it out.

"And what do you want?" I asked him. He sat chewing thoughtfully for a moment.

"I want my mother to shut up about it, and leave me alone." I laughed, which made him smile. He seemed to relax a bit, and we started chatting about our university days.

When he relaxed and dropped the scowl, he was really sexy. I began to speculate about what he'd be like in bed. Would he be buttoned up and conventional, or an uninhibited tiger? My belly squeezed just thinking about it.

"What did you think of Ivan?" He asked, breaking my erotic thoughts.

"Charismatic, handsome. Sly bugger though. Apparently all the girls in the office fancy him."

"And do you?"

"I have my hands full here," I flirted, which made him smile again.

"Charmer. Seriously, do you fancy him?"

"No. I can appreciate that he's handsome, but it's never good when you know they can't be trusted. I watched him in action, remember. Anyway, I heard he only likes supermodels, so that rules me out."

"Oh I don't know, you're the prettiest lawyer I've ever met. I know he was desperate to find out more about you."

"And you called me a charmer. He can find out what he likes, it doesn't change the fact that he was trying to scam our client." I wanted to close down the conversation. Knowing he was a friend of Ivan's, I didn't want to give any indication that I was in any way enamoured. I changed the subject, "so how come you're still single? There must be loads of socialites and models desperate to hang off your arm?"

"They bore me. When there's not much going on upstairs, the downstairs loses its allure pretty fast," he said, his face impassive, "and how come you're still single?"

"I work too hard, long hours don't always go down well with boyfriends." It wasn't entirely the truth, as I had deliberately kept the south London lads at arms length, not wanting two babies by age eighteen, and my feet nailed to the floor. Again, I couldn't share that one.

"Unless you're with someone ambitious, they don't get it do they?" Oscar had hit the nail on the head. The boys I had grown up with aspired to be gas fitters and postmen, and do as little work as they could get away with, preferring to spend their time in the pub instead. I looked over at Oscar, chairman of a bank, the right age, and extraordinarily handsome, and decided I needed to play my A game.

"No they don't. I figured that any man who didn't appreciate my career and work ethic wouldn't be right for me, so it was better to stay single than settle for second best."

We spent the rest of the meal talking about our jobs, current affairs and other easy subjects. Oscar paid the bill, and we headed outside where another taxi was waiting for us. Back at the flats, he travelled up in the lift with me to the top floor.

"Would you like a coffee?" I offered, having made the decision that only coffee would be the agenda that night. He came in and sat at the kitchen island while I made us both lattes.

"This flat really is lovely, I wish I'd bought it," he said, looking around.

"Isn't yours the same?"

"Similar, this one has a different layout though, mine isn't as open plan. It had to have more walls with another flat built over it. I usually only stay there during the week, so it's not a big deal."

"Where do you live at the weekend then?"

"I have a place in Sussex. I usually go Friday night and come back Monday morning, but last weekend I had a social engagement, and this weekend, a date with you."

We finished our coffees, and I yawned, "I'm gonna have to send you home, I've had a lovely evening, and thank you for dinner." We both stood up, and I walked round the island to see him out. He slid his arms around my waist, crushing me to his chest. Briefly he gazed at my face, as if he was trying to work me out, before he leaned down to kiss me gently, his lips grazing mine before becoming more urgent. His tongue ran across my lower lip before it met mine, in lush, soft licks. He smelled fabulous up close, and as his hands roamed over my back, everything south of my waist tightened viciously. Not shagging him was going to take every bit of resolve I possessed. After a minute, I pulled away. He smiled a lovely crooked smile.

"Are you sure you want me to go?"

"Yes, I need some sleep." I caught a look of annoyance flash over his face, but it was fleeting.

"As you wish, can I take you out to breakfast tomorrow morning?"

"Ok. What time?"

"Nine?" I nodded in reply, before opening the front door for him. He gave me another quick kiss on the lips before disappearing into the lift. I closed the door and leaned against it to cool my heated back. I was in big trouble where Oscar Golding was concerned.

I headed off to bed, wondering if he would be playing the maudlin music again. I lay in the dark straining my ears, but couldn't hear a sound. The thought of him laying just one floor below me, possibly naked, had me reaching for my battery-operated-boyfriend to help me get to sleep.

I woke up early the next day. It didn't seem to matter what time I went to bed, I always woke at the same time. I decided to go to the gym to kill some time before my breakfast date. By eight I was back home, showered, and my hair done. I decided to wear black jeans that flattered my bum, and a thin, loose, blue jumper, which hung slightly off one shoulder and draped nicely over my bust. At nine precisely, there was a knock at the front door. I opened it to find Oscar leaning lazily against the door jamb wearing Levi's and a grey t shirt. He looked just as gorgeous in casual clothes as he did in a suit.

He kissed me on the cheek, and waited while I grabbed my handbag and keys. As soon as we were out of the lift, he grabbed my hand, and we walked round to the arcade in the sunshine. He led me to a little cafe where we ordered full English each, and lattes. He looked younger in jeans, and almost carefree compared to the snarling, uptight, unhappy person I had pegged him as at first. I settled back into my chair and relaxed. Our food arrived, looking tempting, and my stomach grumbled in anticipation. We tucked in.

"Sleep well?" Oscar said, breaking the companionable silence.

"Great thanks. You?" I replied, more to be polite than anything.

"I would have slept better if I hadn't spent the evening being teased. Why did you send me home Elle?" *What? Did he seriously expect me to shag him on the first date?*

"I beg your pardon? It was the first time we spent an evening together. What did you expect me to do?"

"Is that your only issue? That it was our first date?"

I blushed a bit, "Oscar, that's a bit direct. Yes, I don't have sex on the first date." He looked thoughtful as he ate a piece of egg and bacon.

"So does this count as a second date? I won't beat about the bush Elle, I need to fuck you, so just tell me what you want me to do, and we can cut the crap."

Those crude words coming out of Oscars sculptured mouth in his cut crystal accent, shocked me. My forkful of sausage hovered in the air while I considered my response.

"I'm guessing the 'I need to fuck you' approach has a high success rate for you," I said, trying not to look horribly offended.

"Well, we are both adults," he said, his impassive mask back on. I put down my knife and fork, and leaned forward.

"I am deciding whether or not I want to fuck you, not when I want to fuck you," I replied, "you'd do well to remember that." *Yay! Go me!*

"If you think that keeping me waiting is going to make me chase you, then I can tell you now, you're wrong. I don't subscribe to the bourgeois point of view of making a man wait. If you don't fancy me, then I'd rather you say now than spend time pointlessly hanging around."

I stared at him, shocked at his bluntness. His eyes were cold and steely, and his face impassive. The thought struck me that he was behaving like a spoilt child who had never heard the word no. His attempt to manipulate me into shagging him to stop him walking away was juvenile and misguided. There was no way I'd be railroaded into bed for fear of losing someone. I popped the last bit of toast in my mouth and quickly swallowed. As sad as I was not to witness Oscar naked, there was no way I was prepared to shag him in the hope of stopping him walking away. I pulled a twenty out of my purse and slapped it down on the table.

"I don't expect you to hang around. Consider my mind made up," I hissed, before I stomped off. His face was a mixture of astonishment and anger, but he didn't come after me.

Rather than head back to the flat where I might bump into him, I headed over to the West End, to walk through Hyde park, and gather my thoughts, or rather, sulk. I found a bench in a quiet corner of the park and sat down. It was a glorious spring day, and the tulips swayed gently in the warm breeze. I took a few deep, cleansing breaths. They didn't work, and a large tear rolled down my cheek. I swiped it away angrily, cross with myself for getting upset. Oscar was way out of my league, and I had known that from the start. It had been the reason I had been guarded about letting him have my body, as I had known he would never have been able to love someone like me. *You're being suburban, Elle, men like Oscar don't love, they make alliances, and wanting to be loved pegs you as the working class girl you want to escape. Woman up.*

As I let the self pity wash over me, my phone chirped. Pulling it out my bag, I saw immediately it was a text from James.

hey little Elle, how was the date? Hope your ok. All good here

I smiled as I tapped out my reply;

hey big James, got dumped already, am ok, glad it's goin well out there. Miss you.

My phone rang about a minute later.

"What do you mean you got dumped?" James said without preamble.

"I didn't shag him, so he said I was bourgeois and said he'd walk away if I didn't, so I left. I thought he was too good to be true," I sniffed.

"Elle are you crying? A tosser like that should most definitely not make you cry. Sounds like you had a lucky escape to me. Everyone knows a lady doesn't shag on the first date."

"That's what I thought, anyway, how are the yanks treating you?"

"Great. They want to buy my app. I have clear direction on how Apple want it constructed, and I'm meeting a couple of banks in New York in the next few days to get their input. Oh, and they put me up in the most amazing hotel."

"Email me some pictures please? I need cheering up."

"Will do, and Elle? You are too good for an idiot man who doesn't realise he can't click his fingers and make demands. You're better than that, don't forget it."

I smiled as we said our goodbyes. James had only been gone a day, and I missed him already. By the time I had walked back to Hyde Park corner, I was in a much better mood. I decided to forget Oscar Golding, and carry on being New Elle, who had a great job, and fabulous life. I wasn't going to be beaten that easily.

I headed home around five, picking up some groceries on the way. There was no sign of Oscar in the lobby, and I was grateful to reach my front door without incident. As I closed the door behind me, I noticed an envelope on the floor. It was expensive cream vellum, and just had my name handwritten on the front. Knowing who it was from, I placed it on the kitchen island as I made my coffee, and put the groceries away. I sat and turned it over in my hands before garnering the courage to open it.

Dear Elle,
I'm so sorry about the way I behaved today. I was crass and demanding, and I don't blame you for walking away. I hope you can forgive me, and give me the opportunity to treat you like the lady you undoubtedly are.
Regards
Oscar

I read the note several times. After his assertion that he wouldn't chase, it most definitely felt like round one to me. I smiled, and threw the note down onto the island. The best thing to do now was nothing. I would ignore the note, and ignore Oscar.

I ran a deep, luxurious bath, adding a few drops of a free sample of bath oil. I sank in, and lay back, feeling the tension in my body relax

Chapter 4

Re-writing the contract was the priority first thing Monday morning. Lewis asked me to assist him, and together we sat going through line by line. The clients and Ivan were meeting again at two, so we worked like demons to get it done and ready. At twelve, we were interrupted by Priti.

"Elle, Oscar Goldings at the front desk. Are you breaking for lunch, or should I tell him you're busy?"

"Can you tell him I'm busy please. Doubt if we'll get time for lunch today."

"Will do," she said as she headed back out. I put it out of my mind, and concentrated on my work.

Our clients arrived at quarter to two, and sat in the conference room as Lewis explained the revised contract. By five to, they were briefed and happy, and waiting in anticipation for Ivan. He arrived bang on time, and yet again my brain fried slightly at the sight of him. He stared at me pointedly, before taking his seat at the large table. Lewis presented him with a copy of the revised contract, which he read quickly. We had already emailed a copy to his legal team about an hour previously, so I presumed he was in agreement with the revised figures.

This time, he spoke very little, and his lawyer did the talking. With both sides in agreement, they all signed, shook hands, and the deal was done. There was a bit of relief in the air as all the men began to file out of the conference room. I was packing up my papers as a loud, Russian voice boomed out.

"Miss Reynolds, I would like to speak to you alone please." My head whipped up to see Ivan fixing me with his intense stare.

"Sure," I said, "here ok?" He nodded, and waited for the rest of the men to leave, Lewis giving me a raised eyebrow as he left. Ivan walked over to the door and closed it, before turning to face me.

"You are very impressive for such a young woman," he said. *Sexist bastard.*

"Thanks.......is that all?" I said brightly, hoping to shut him down. He was making me nervous. The way he looked at me reminded me of a cat looking at a mouse. *Predator.*

"No. You intrigue me Ms Reynolds. Do I intrigue you?"

"Mr Porenski, it's not something I've given any thought to. Now is there anything else? I have a full schedule to be getting back to."

"Would you have dinner with me tonight?" He looked at me expectantly.

"No, I'm sorry but I'm busy." As soon as I said it, I regretted it a little. Ivan was the grand prize, the one everyone wanted. I just didn't feel up to handling another alpha male so soon after spending a day feeling like crap.

"Oscar was a fool to let you slip away from him. I wouldn't make the same mistake. Now, Elle, take a good, long look at me, and tell me if you see a man who takes no for an answer." *Smug git.*

"No means no. I have no idea what Oscar did or didn't tell you, but when I say no I mean it. Do yourself a favour, and accept it gracefully." My voice was a little louder than I wanted, but I was annoyed, a bit humiliated that they had discussed me, and deeply offended that they both seemed to think a wallet waved in my face would make my knickers fall down.

"Are you this much of a tiger between the sheets?" Ivan chuckled, which enraged me further. I grabbed my papers, and stalked out. The only place I could go where he couldn't follow was the ladies, so I hurried in, and hid in the loo.

About fifteen minutes later, Priti came in, calling me. I sheepishly unlocked the door, and came out.

"It's alright, Ivan's gone. What on earth happened?"

"Long story. The mans a pig, and so is Oscar. I don't want to see either of them right now." I washed my hands and pulled myself together.

"So you have the two hottest men on the planet both hanging round you like puppies, and you want me to say 'poor Elle, must be terrible'. Are you mad? Your a lucky, lucky bitch." She bumped shoulders with me, and we both laughed.

"When you put it like that...." I smiled. Even though both men scared me, and had offended me, it was still a bit of an ego boost.

I went back to my office, braced for the inevitable ribbing I would get. All that happened was Lewis poking his head round the door to ask if I was ok. The other three men seemingly engrossed in fascinating work on their screens. I carried on working till around seven, before my stomach interrupted me with some loud grumbling. I switched off my screen and headed home.

Back at the flat, I microwaved a meal for one, again missing James, and switched on the telly. I changed into some fleece pyjamas, and settled down on the sofa for a quiet night. A loud knock at the door made me jump. Rather than open it, I called out "who is it?"

"Who do you think?" *Bugger, piss off Oscar, I'm not in the mood.*

"Not now Oscar. I'm busy."

"Is someone with you?"

"Nope."

"Then open the door. I won't keep you long." I sighed and opened the door. He smiled tentatively as I stood aside to let him in. If he noticed my unsexy jimjams, he didn't comment. I made us both coffee, and we sat at the island. I looked at him, waiting to hear what he had to say. His eyes flicked down to the discarded note, before looking back at me.

"I really need to apologise for Sunday morning," he said, "I behaved like a boor, and prat. I don't normally go around trying to bully women for sex. I'm sorry."

"Apology accepted. You need to know that I won't be bullied. So why did you say those things to me?" He took a deep breath.

"Women don't say no to me, as a rule."

"Really? Wow. You must find low self esteem attractive in a woman then." He tried to fight a smile.

"Not particularly, but in general, most women think I'm attractive."

"I never said you weren't attractive, I just like to be sure I'm giving my body to someone who appreciates it. If you just want a quick shag, pretty much every secretary in my office would be happy to oblige."

"That's not what I'm after. I think you know that by now."

"Hmm. I'm not sure I do. I didn't appreciate being made to feel like a bourgeois little girl who was attempting to manipulate you. I'm sad that you felt that way."

"I don't, I just didn't realise how little the title and accoutrements would mean to you. Most women are overwhelmed by it all. Like I said before, I don't as a rule chase women, I don't really need to, but here I am, begging forgiveness." He looked contrite.

"Ok, forgiven, just don't do it again." I smiled at him, unsure what was going to happen next.

"Ivan told me you turned him down today. You need to be careful, people don't say no to him very often either."

I shrugged, "I'm sure he'll get over it, and move quickly on to a model or socialite. I couldn't see a date with him being much fun."

"True, he probably gets his bodyguards to frisk his dates to check for weapons before he kisses them goodnight. He's a bit paranoid about security." Oscar smiled, relieved, I thought, that Ivan hadn't impressed me.

He hopped off his stool and came around the island, his arms held out for a hug. He stood between my knees, and wrapped his arms around me, "friends again?" He asked.
"Yep, friends again," I replied. Hesitantly, he grazed my lips with his, and seeing I didn't pull away, he brushed across my lips again, before deepening the kiss. He tasted of coffee and Oscar, a heady combination, and one that made my entire body respond to him. As I relaxed into his arms, he pulled me closer, crushing me against his chest, his hands roaming over my pyjama clad back.

"You're not wearing a bra," he groaned, pressing little kisses along my jaw. In a moment of extraordinary bravery, and turned on beyond belief at his close proximity, I took a deep breath.

"I'm not wearing any knickers either." He drew in a sharp breath, and rested his forehead against mine.

"Please," was all he said. I pulled away, and hopped down from the stool. Taking his hand, I led him into my bedroom.

Oscar carried on kissing me as he undid the little buttons of my pyjama top. He slipped it off my shoulders, and let it fall to the floor. Pulling away from me slightly, he stared at my naked breasts, "exquisite," was all he said, before running his hands over them. He pulled his shirt off quickly, and crushed me to his bare chest for another luscious, deep, kiss. Bending down, he took one of my nipples in his mouth, and flicked it with his tongue, while pinching the other with his fingers. It sent my state of arousal soaring, and at that moment, he could have been Bluebeard himself, and I would still have begged him to fuck me. His hand slipped down my pyjama bottoms, and he groaned as he felt how ready I was. He slid his finger backward and forward over my clit as his tongue worked on my nipple.

"Please," I begged, desperate to feel him inside me. I reached for his waistband, and, with trembling fingers, undid his trousers, and pulled them down. He did the same to me, and pushed me back gently onto the bed. I could see an impressive erection straining through his jersey boxers. Kicking off the last of his clothes, he rifled through the pockets of his trousers to find his wallet, and pull a condom from it. I ogled him unashamedly as he unrolled the condom over his large dick, and crawled up the bed towards me.

His face was flushed as he pushed two fingers inside me, and massaged my clit with his thumb, all the time watching my face.

"You're such a dirty girl, I can feel how wet and greedy your cunt is," he said, shocking me. The crude words spoken in his cut glass accent, sounded beyond carnal.

"I need you inside me, I'm gonna come soon. Please Oscar," I begged, as at that point I didn't give a toss how dirty he wanted to talk. He positioned himself over me, and slammed into me hard, hitting that sweet spot that lies between pain and pleasure. He began to thrust into me, angling his body so that his large cock could stroke my g spot over and over again. I began to feel the familiar quivering sensation of an impending orgasm. He must have felt it too.

"Come on, come all over my cock you dirty bitch," he hissed, just before I came hard, everything blotted out during an overwhelming orgasm. "Your cunt is milking me dry," he gasped, before shuddering at his own release.

We lay there a while, him still inside me, as we caught our breath, and came down from our orgasms. He kissed me softly on the lips before pulling out, and flopping down beside me.

"You are every bit as sexy as I thought you'd be," he said while he tied a knot in the condom. I lay back and contemplated the sex, it had been great, and he was pretty skilled, but in hindsight his crude words had been unexpected and a bit jarring.

"So you like to talk dirty? That was unexpected." I was probing. He turned to face me, propping himself on his elbow as he smoothed my hair off my face in a tender gesture.

"Did it bother you?"

"Just sounded strange, crude words in a posh accent."

He laughed, and tweaked my nipple. He looked boyish, and a bit smug. "I can't help my accent anymore than you can help yours. Do I sound ridiculous when I talk dirty then?"

I smiled back, "no, I just expect it. So do slutty, dirty girls turn you on?" I looked down at his dick, which was hardening again. *Round two? Quick reload there Oscar.*

I leaned down to suck and lick his nipple, licking the silky warm skin of his torso. He lay back, running his fingers through my hair, sending little shivers through me. I pressed little kisses over his tummy, and slowly worked my way down to his erection, which was back to full strength. I kissed and licked the tip, before taking it fully into my mouth, and working my lips up and down the shaft.

"Oh god, Elle, that feels fantastic," he murmured. I kissed, licked and sucked every inch of his beautiful cock and balls, driving him crazy.

"Condoms, have you got condoms?" He panted.

"Top drawer," I muttered against the tip of his cock. He shifted slightly, and fumbled around to find the foil packet. As soon as it was on, he pulled me on top of him. I straddled him, and lowered myself onto his cock, groaning at the exquisite fullness, as he stretched me inside. Oscar licked his finger, and ran it gently over my clit as I moved slowly up and down, trying to prolong my orgasm as long as I could.

"So is this what you like, dirty boy?" I whispered, as I rode him deliberately slower and slower. He garbled something unintelligible before shouting his release. I quickly followed, and could only sit helpless as my body pulsed and shook around him.

Afterwards, he pulled me into a deep kiss, crushing me against his chest, his strong hands caressing my back.

"You are so beautiful," he sighed, "you know I'm going to want to fuck you again in about half an hour."

"You're insatiable." He looked pleased with himself. "Would you like a drink while I'm waiting?"

He grinned, "coffee would be good. I need a shot of caffeine if I'm gonna be up all night satisfying you." I clambered off him, and threw his shirt on to go and make our drinks.

We made love once more that night, before drifting off to sleep. I woke up to find Oscar wrapped around me, his arm across my chest, and one of his legs curved around mine. He looked younger as he slept, his face peaceful and relaxed. I managed to slither out of bed without disturbing him, and went to the kitchen to make a drink. Feeling as stiff as a board, and for want of a better phrase, well used, I made the decision to forego the gym that morning.

I took a coffee in to Oscar, and gently nudged him awake. "Morning sleepyhead, time to get up," I said, stroking his shoulder. He opened sleepy blue eyes, and stretched.

"Good morning beautiful, are you waking me up for round four?"

"No. I'm waking you up because I need to get ready for work. It's half six already."

"God, you get up early. I don't normally start until nine thirty. Shall I come and scrub your back?" He looked at me suggestively.

"That won't be necessary, but I do need to get ready. I go in at half seven."

He slid out of bed and wandered into my bathroom, "I'm exhausted. Not sure what you did to me last night, but I can't remember the last time I was this wrung out," he called out. He reappeared in my room, and pulled his clothes on. "Daft question, considering, but can I have your phone number?" I scribbled it down for him as he finished his coffee, and he left, with a parting 'I'll call you.'

I went into work feeling chipper, and excited to have finally got it together with gorgeous Oscar. Nothing was going to ruin my good mood, even Lewis assigning me the most boring merger that ever happened as my project for the rest of the week. I fully expected Oscar to ask me for lunch, so when I walked into the foyer at twelve, I was surprised that he wasn't there. Frowning slightly, I joined Priti in the lift down to the arcade for a sandwich.

The afternoon saw radio silence too. I headed home around six, expecting a call, or a visit. I must have checked my phone twenty times that evening. Nothing. By the end of the following day, the realisation dawned, *I'd been had.* Oscar had gone all out to fuck me, nothing more. Once I'd shagged him, he lost interest. *What a stupid girl.*

I consoled myself with the knowledge that I'd had some great sex, and nobody else knew about it, especially the people at work. My humiliation would be a secret only Oscar and I shared.

Chapter 5

By Thursday morning, I was reconciled to the fact that Oscar had lost interest. I had gone back to my routines, and was missing James terribly. He was due back Saturday afternoon, and it couldn't come soon enough for me. I was lonely in the flat without him, and missed his company, and cooking.

I was at my desk, going through a contract, when I heard the buzz of excitement on the main floor. Shortly afterwards, Matt wandered in, grinning.

"The Ruskies back in Elle, better make yourself scarce, he looked hungry today."

"What times he due out of his meeting?"

"About an hour."

An hour later I made myself scarce, again, hiding in the ladies. I stayed for ten minutes before checking the coast was clear, and slinking back to my desk.

"He came in to look for you," Matt said cheerfully, "and left you this." He handed me a note.

Elle,
I'm still thinking about you. Call me on 07985 267485 and tell me where you would like me to take you for dinner.
Ivan

I tucked the note in my handbag as Matt watched me expectantly. I ignored him, and settled back down at my desk, picking up the infernally boring merger contract. I must have read the same line four times, before admitting to myself that I was struggling to concentrate. I decided it was a good time to break for

46

lunch, clear my head, and pull myself together. I tidied my papers, and grabbed my handbag, before walking through to reception.

Oscar stood by the main desk, talking to Priti. They both looked up as I walked towards them, Oscar smiling widely.

"Hello Elle, thought I'd join you for lunch today. It's been a mad busy week, and this is the first chance I've had." He held his hand out for me to take, and not knowing quite what to do, I took it.

When we were out of earshot of Prit, I turned to him, "I thought you were meant to call me."

"I was, but I've been working a lot, and had meetings in the city the last two nights. I didn't think you'd appreciate being a late night booty call."

"You're right there."

He took me to a little bistro in the arcade, and found us a table. After we had ordered, he sat, playing with my fingers across the table.

"Can I see you tonight? We can go out or something, only I'm gonna be away this weekend, and I don't want to wait another week."

I relaxed. Busy I could understand. "You could have text me. I thought you didn't want to see me anymore." *Why did I say that? Elle, you are being needy, snap out of it girl.*

"Why would I not want to see you? I thought we had a great time together." Oscar looked affronted.

"Yeah, we did." I smiled at him, trying to forget two days of wondering why he hadn't called.

"You could always come to Sussex with me this weekend. I don't have anything going on down there. Next weekend would be better as I've got a bunch of friends coming to stay for a weekend shoot."

"James is back Saturday, and I'd really like to be there. Next weekend sounds fun, but I don't shoot."

"I'll teach you. I'm having about ten people stay. We shoot clay pigeons, then get drunk. It'll be a blast."

"Ok, next weekend it is then."

Our food arrived, and we began to eat. Oscar looked thoughtful. He put his fork down and stared at me. "This thing with James, you are just friends?"

"Of course we're just friends, or rather, flatmates. I have no interest in him sexually, and I don't think he sees me that way either. He's a nice guy, and a good friend, that's all." Oscar seemed satisfied with my answer, and resumed eating.

We chatted easily for the rest of our meal. Oscar seemed to have loosened up around me, and made me laugh with his impression of the pompous arses he had dinner with at mansion house the previous evening. I went back to work considerably more cheerful, and got my head down to work without further issue.

He picked me up at half seven that evening, and took me to Ronnie Scott's. we had a gorgeous meal, and I discovered that Oscar was an extremely good dancer. His lithe, muscular body moved gracefully and sensually in time to the music.

When a slow song came on, he drew me close, and pressed his body against mine as we swayed in time to the music.

"Shall we go after this?" He whispered in my ear. I nodded in reply. His warm body and wonderful scent already had me turned on and ready. We hopped into a taxi, and went straight back to my flat. He began unbuttoning my blouse in the lift on the way up, laughing as I slapped his hands away. We tumbled into the flat, passionately kissing and pulling at clothes. I was half naked by the time we stumbled into my bedroom, and fell onto the bed. Oscar practically ripped my remaining clothes off, then quickly shed his own, before crawling naked up my body to kiss me fiercely once more.

"I have to get inside you Elle, I'm gonna explode. It's all I've thought of the last few days," Oscar murmured as he kissed my jaw. He slid on a condom, and thrust inside me. Precisely three thrusts later, Oscar cursed.

"Fuck, sorry Elle, just too turned on."

He pulled out, and rolled onto his back, removing the condom, before staring at the ceiling.

"It's fine, I'm sure you'll be ready again in a few minutes," I cooed, rubbing my thighs together to get some friction. I fully expected him to carry on with either his fingers or his mouth, but he just lay there.

"Oscar, I haven't come yet," I said, trying to prompt him.

"Christ, will you just give me a minute," he snapped, effectively pouring a bucket of cold water over my arousal. I jumped out of bed and threw on a robe.

"It's fine, but I think you need to go home to sleep," I said, desperate to get rid of him, "don't forget I get up early."

"Thought you wanted another shag," he said, looking at me apprehensively.

"I've gone off the idea," I said, picking his clothes up from the floor, and laying them on the end of the bed.

"What's got into you? I just came in five seconds flat, which is embarrassing, and I need a few minutes before I can go again. Is that really so unusual?"

"There's no need to shout at me. You could have used your hands or your mouth to bring me off. You wouldn't like it if I left you hanging, then snapped at you for expecting an orgasm."

I turned to pick up a stray sock, and felt a pair of arms around my shoulders. Oscar pulled me backwards, and threw me onto the bed. Pinning me with his body, he glared at me.

"So this greedy little cunt didn't get it's own way tonight? I bet your clit's begging to be rubbed, and have my big cock pounding it."

"Stop it. Please Oscar, stop this now. This is not what I want," I shouted. My emotions were a horrible mixture of anger, fear and embarrassment. "I wanted an orgasm, not raping, and you're scaring me." I let out a sob.

"Elle, stop, I'm so sorry baby. I didn't mean to frighten you, I thought you were playing." Oscar looked horrified at the tears rolling down my face. He immediately pulled off me, and wrapped his arms around me, holding me tightly. "Baby, please forgive me. I would never, ever hurt you. Please stop crying." He began to press little kisses along my jaw. I pulled back to look at him. He looked uncertain and contrite as he gazed back. Wiping my tear streaked face with a corner of the sheet, he smiled tentatively.

"I'm so sorry baby, please forgive me. Now would you prefer that orgasm, or would you rather I went home?" He traced around my nipple as he said it, sparking my already sensitised body. I didn't reply, just pulling him into a deep kiss.

His hand slid down to palm my clitoris, before he slipped two fingers inside me, gently pumping them back and forth. His mouth enveloped my nipple with heat, his tongue causing a spike of pleasure that travelled straight down to my groin. I ran my fingers through his thick hair, and over the satiny skin of his back. He groaned.

"Please, I want you inside me," I begged shamelessly. He grabbed a condom, and within seconds, was nudging into me.

This time, he moved slowly, changing angles to stroke every inch of my insides, and wring as much pleasure as possible from our lovemaking. He caressed my breasts as he kept his deliciously slow pace, murmuring over and over how beautiful he thought I was.

Whether it was the effects of being denied an earlier orgasm, or just his slow, exact pace, but the orgasm I felt brewing inside me threatened to rip me apart. He must have felt my insides quivering, because he pinched my nipples at exactly the right moment. I came with a scream, unable to do anything except lay helplessly as everything inside me pulled tight and pulsed mercilessly.

He watched me come, his expression inscrutable. After the waves of my climax subsided, he came with a shout, his body shuddering as he let go. He kissed me passionately before pulling out and laying beside me propped up on his elbow.

"That better?"

"Much," I said, "but what was that all about earlier?"

He shrugged. "Embarrassed about coming so quick I guess. I haven't suffered premature ejaculation since I was a teenager."

"Have you slept with many women?" I was curious. He eyed me suspiciously.

"Probably about average for my age," he answered evasively, "how many men have you slept with?"

"Only three in my entire life, including you." He looked stunned.

"How come?"

I shrugged, "same boy through college, one while I was doing my traineeship. I was never into the whole sleeping around thing, plus, as I said before, my focus has been my career."

Oscar snuggled into me after I turned the light off, kissing my shoulder softly. I drifted off into a dreamless sleep, feeling surprisingly comfortable against the warmth and hardness of his body.

The following morning, Oscar dragged himself out of bed and downstairs, dutifully, at six, so I could get myself off to the gym at my usual time. Before he left, he invited me up to his office for lunch. As he would be in Sussex all weekend, it comforted me to know I wasn't being treated as a once a week shag. Meeting at his office seemed to elevate me towards girlfriend status, which made me happy. I practically skipped to the gym.

The morning seemed to last forever. I was still working on the boring merger, so I threw myself into checking everything line by line to try and take my mind off how slowly the clock was moving. The only mildly exciting event was being invited out for Friday night drinks by the men I shared the office with. Matt explained that most of the lawyers met at 'Lauren's bar' every Friday after work, and as I was no longer the newbie, I was invited.

Finally, five to twelve came around, and I headed up in the lifts. Goldings bank took an entire two floors in the tower, being a major player in corporate finance. I smoothed the front of my dress as I strode towards the ornate reception desk, taking in the artwork on the walls and plush furnishings of the foyer area.

"I'm meeting Oscar Golding for lunch, my name's Elle Reynolds."

The receptionist was a glacial blonde, who stared down her nose at me before replying, "Lord Golding's office is expecting you. Please follow me."

It took me a moment to twig what she had said. *What was The Lord thing all about?* I trotted along behind her as she led me down a thickly carpeted corridor. At the end were large, wooden double doors, with a brass plaque with 'Lord Golding' engraved on it. She paused before knocking.

"Come in," Oscar's voice called out. Glacial blonde opened the door, and stood aside to let me in. Oscar stood up and bounded round his desk, his arms out. He kissed my cheek, and lightly hugged me. Glacial blonde coughed.

"Will that be all sir?" She asked, eyeing me strangely.

"Yes thank you. I'll call if we need anything," he said, dismissing her, before grasping my hand and leading me to a large table with two salvers on it, and two glasses of white wine. "I'm so glad you could come. I didn't want to go a whole three days till I can see you again," he smiled, and lifted the silver lids off of our lunches. He'd arranged poached salmon salads for us, which looked appetising. I opened the napkin, but before I began my food, I had to ask the burning question.

"I didn't know you were a Lord. Why didn't you tell me?"

He paused, and looked thoughtful. "I thought you'd google me, and when it was clear you had no idea, I kinda liked it. Probably sounds odd, but you fancied Oscar Golding the man, rather than Lord Golding, the bank chairman. Most women I meet instantly start fantasising about becoming Lady Golding." He began to eat.

"The only title I've ever aspired to is 'your honour', and that's unlikely given my specialism. Did you google me?"

"I tried, but not much came up. Only your stuff at Pearson and Hardwick. How come you're not on the social networks?"

"Not into all that stuff. Plus I stare at screens all day, I'm not doing it for fun as well. Why are you nosing into my lack of desire to spread the minutiae of my life on the Internet?" I asked sweetly.

"I thought all women were on Facebook. Ivan ordered a full background check on you. I haven't gone that far, you'll be pleased to know."

"What did he uncover?"

"No idea. I didn't ask, and I think he's smarting at being turned down, so he's not mentioned you since." I breathed a sigh of relief. I didn't want my humble beginnings being an issue at this stage.

We had a lovely lunch. Oscar was adorable and fun. When my hour was up, he pulled me into his arms and kissed me passionately before walking me to the lift with his arm flung casually around my shoulders, which caused Glacial Blonde to scowl and shoot me a daggers look.

"She has a crush on you," I whispered outside the foyer.

"Nah, boss complex," he dismissed, smirking, "anyway, I have my hands full. I wish you were coming with me this weekend though. I won't see you now till next week."

"I know, but I'm sure you'll have a nice weekend. See you next week" I said, before he pressed a chaste kiss to my lips. I went back to work with a big smile on my face.

At half five we all packed up and went down to the bar. Matt and Adrian grabbed a table while Peter and I waited at the bar. As the newbie, I bought the first round. With their ties loosened, I discovered that the men I shared an office with were good company. Some of the other lawyers joined us, and I began to relax and enjoy myself. There were very few female lawyers in the company, and they were all much older, and not inclined to go drinking after work, so I was the only female in our crowd. I got teased mercilessly about having to hide in the loo whenever Ivan appeared, and they all appeared impressed that I hadn't succumbed to the Russian's charms.

"So are you seeing Oscar Golding then?" Adrian asked.

"Yeah, I've been out with him a couple of times."

"Shagged him yet?"

"Nosy bastard aren't you?"

"You have!" Adrian shouted. I stayed silent. I didn't want to say either way. "That bastard has it with jam on. Owns a bank, titled, rich, good looking. Please don't tell me he has a big dick too."

I blushed, feeling the blood creep up my face. "No comment." They all laughed. The banter was all good natured, and the conversation soon turned to weekend plans. I found out that Matt was a member of the TA, and was training, Adrian was travelling to Brighton to visit his parents, and Peter was planning an Ikea trip with his girlfriend as they had recently bought a house. One by one, everyone left. I chatted to some of the other lawyers for a while before saying my goodbyes and strolling home.

Chapter 6

The next morning, after my workout, I cleaned the flat and filled the fridge ready for James' return. I had really missed him, considering I hadn't known him that long. He arrived home at tea time, exhausted and jet lagged from the flight, so I made us both coffee and some dinner, and we sat down to discuss his trip. He described all the meetings, the people he'd met, and the places he'd stayed. It sounded like he had been accommodated in five star style, and been courted by some major players.

"They gave me a contract to sign. Would you mind going over it for me?"

"Course not, I'll check it for you. Saves you paying a lawyer." I didn't mind doing that for James, he'd been good to me. He pulled the contract out of his rucksack, and plopped it onto the island. I scanned it quickly. It looked pretty detailed, and I wanted to make sure James was happy with what he was signing up to.

"We need to go through this together, line by line, to make sure you know exactly what this contract entails. Shall we earmark tomorrow for it?"

James groaned, "if we must. I feel a bit shattered right now, but I'm trying to stay awake to get back to a normal sleep pattern. I need more coffee, I'm dropping off already." I made us both more coffee, and told James a rather edited version of my week. He looked amused at my stories about the dates I was taken on by Oscar, raising his eyebrows at the lunch-in-his-office date.

"He sounds very taken with you. I still think you need to be careful around him though. There really is something about him that puts me on edge. I don't mean that I think he's a paedo or anything like that, more a sort of.....coldness. I can't imagine him being kind to small animals, that type of thing."

"I know exactly what you mean. He certainly doesn't like being challenged, and no, I can't see him liking kittens either."

"Unless they're in a sandwich." We both laughed, which felt a bit disloyal to Oscar, but James had hit the nail on the head. I knew Oscar fancied me, I knew he found me attractive, but I didn't know whether he actually liked me, let alone developed deeper feelings. For my part, I liked him, enjoyed his company, but still felt intimidated and unsure around him. I fancied the pants off the man though, so had buried my disquiet, putting it down to my own insecurities about my background. I told James that I was going to Oscar's place in Sussex next weekend. He just raised his eyebrows.

"Best develop a thirst for blood sports, and grow a thick skin this week then little Elle. I think you may need it. More coffee?"

"Please. I won't lie, I'm worried about not fitting in, but if Oscar thinks it'll be fine, then all I can do is go along with it." James had voiced my fears, but in truth, I would have been more worried if Oscar had wanted to keep me a secret. The fact that he wanted to introduce me to his friends was a step forward as far as I was concerned.

Despite all the coffee, James was in bed by nine. Poor man couldn't keep his eyes open. I tidied up the kitchen before taking a long bath to contemplate what lay ahead.

Going through the contract took the whole of Sunday morning. It was extremely detailed and precise, but there were a couple of clauses that James wasn't happy with, namely a severe anti competition clause that would prevent him building any more apps for a year. I suggested he get it changed so that he could still build games and lifestyle apps, and agree not to build financial ones. I also picked up on a percentage issue, as the apps would be given away free by the respective banks, they wanted one payment, with no further cost per download. I suggested we negotiate a nominal amount to provide residual income. I drafted an email for him, asking for the changes, and explaining what was acceptable. James breathed a sigh of relief once the email was sent.

"Thanks Elle, I wouldn't have spotted any of that without you. Now, shall I take you out for Sunday lunch? I know a great little place on the river."

"No problem. Glad to help. A roast sounds like a great idea." We grabbed our jackets and wandered down towards the river. The restaurant was small and cosy, and we both settled on the roast chicken. Two bottles of wine later, we both wobbled unsteadily back to the flat to sleep off the effects of the enormous dinner, and the copious amounts of alcohol.

Back home, James chose a film, and we flopped down on the sofas to watch. It took about five minutes for James to fall asleep, and I don't think I was too far behind. It was gone six when I woke up, groggy and disorientated. I glanced over at James, who was curled up on the sofa and still out cold. His eyes were flickering behind his eyelids, an indicator of REM sleep. He shifted on the sofa before breathily muttering, "no, please don't." I held my breath as he shifted again. When he seemed to relax again, I slid off the sofa and wandered to the kitchen to pour myself a glass of fruit juice to rehydrate my alcohol parched mouth.

As I padded back through the lounge to my bedroom, James started awake. He scrubbed at his face and stared around the room, clearly as disorientated as I had been.

"Jesus, how long have I been asleep?"

"Couple of hours. I just woke up too, must have been the wine knocked us out. You were talking in your sleep." I swore I saw a hint of a blush on the tiny bit of his face that was visible.

"Bloody hell, what did I say?"

"I'm not sure, but it was something like 'please don't' I have no idea what else you said as I wasn't terribly awake myself."

"I must have been dreaming. God I feel ropey. Why do you let me drink Elle? You know I can't hold my beer." He staggered out of the lounge and headed to his room to the bathroom. A few minutes later, he had his head in the fridge, ferreting around for food, pausing only to finish the orange juice straight from the carton.

He returned with Doritos and dips, which he put on the coffee table for us both. We shared a love of Top Gear, so didn't bother replaying the film, and just sat in companionable silence to watch the Stig.

Monday morning came, and I hit the ground running. I had meetings planned for most of the day, with the first one starting at eight thirty. The morning passed in a blur with no time for lunch. I half expected Oscar to turn up, but was relieved when he didn't, as I had barely time to eat the sandwich one of the assistants brought for me. Mid afternoon, I was just leaving the conference room after a meeting to wrap up the boring merger, when I came face to face with Ivan.

"Miss Reynolds, how lovely to see you," he said in his thickly accented but sexy voice. My knees went slightly weak.

"Mr Porenski, hope you're well. Did you have a good weekend?"

He smiled widely, which opened his face up beautifully, "yes, thank you, I had dinner with Oscar. Such a shame you weren't able to join us."

"Oh, Oscar told me he had nobody coming to stay this weekend. I'm going next weekend though."

"I live a few miles away from his home in Sussex. It's a beautiful place, you'll love it."

"I'd better be getting on, I'm in meetings all day today. Nice to see you Ivan." I scurried away quickly and grabbed some files from my office before heading off to my next meeting, which by coincidence featured Ivan. He was selling a company to a client of ours, and the purpose of the meeting was to form heads of agreement, so that contracts for sale could be drawn up by his legal team.

The meeting went fairly smoothly. Ivan didn't try any bamboozling tactics, and all the basic terms of the deal were agreed in principle without much fuss. As Ivan's legal team had the task of drawing up the contract, we simply had to wait for it to arrive to check that everything was as discussed in the meeting.

As we all stood up to leave, Ivan smiled at me and said, "one day Elle, it would be nice to be on the same side, don't you think?"

I laughed, "engage our company as your lawyers then," before I picked up my files and went back to my office.

I finally made it home by seven thirty that evening, wiped out both mentally and physically by the pace of the day. James had a curry waiting at home, and a large glass of very cold white wine. He was grinning broadly as I walked in.

"They agreed to those terms," he said before I'd even taken my jacket off.

"Yay. You signed now?"

"Ish, they want me to go back out there this Friday, so I can sign everything then."

"Good. Just make sure you check they haven't changed anything else before you ok it."

"Will do. You look shattered. I made us a curry, so sit down and drink your wine while I dish up." I sat down gratefully at the island and took a large gulp of wine. My eyes felt gritty, and my shoulders were up around my neck with tension.

"Elle, there's something I need to tell you," my eyes lifted from my curry to look expectantly at James, "they want me to work out there for the next two or three months. Will you be ok here on your own?"

"I'll be fine. I'll miss you though. Where will you be staying?"

"They said I'll be put up in an apartment in California."

"What a fantastic experience. You grab it with both hands James, and I'll look after everything back here, don't you worry." I felt a sudden pang in my chest. I would miss James more than I wanted to admit. He was a good friend, and we had developed an easy and warm relationship. I cleared away the dinner things, and watched half hour of telly before turning in, noting that Oscar had failed to call.

He turned up at lunchtime the following day, and took me to a little wine bar for lunch. I told him all about James' trip away, and my reservations about being alone in the flat.

"It's very secure there, especially on the high floors. I don't think you need worry about burglars."

"So how was your weekend?

"It was ok. Bit boring really. Ivan came over to dinner on Saturday evening, but apart from that it was just Mother and I. My sister is away in Italy at the moment."

"Your mum lives there?" I was shocked.

"Yes," he said, as if speaking to a small child, "it was her home before I was even born. I inherited it when my father died. I'm hardly going to kick her out now am I? Besides, it's way too big for just one person. At that moment I twigged. We weren't talking about some tiny weekend cottage. "She has an apartment in the East wing. I barely see her to be honest, she's always off doing her WI stuff and charity work. My apartments are in the central part of the house. Well, you'll see on Friday what I mean."

"Ok. I ran into Ivan at work yesterday, he said he went to yours for dinner, that you were neighbours." I took a bite of my sandwich.

"Yes, his estate is about 20 miles from my place. In deepest Sussex, that's a next door neighbour. It's very rural there."

"What clothes will I need?"

Oscar looked at me strangely, "the normal."

"Weekends in the country aren't normal for me, you need to give me a bit more clue than that. I'm a city girl remember?"

"Of course, sorry, jeans and flats for day, party dress for dinner, not long though, cocktail length is fine. We don't stand on ceremony."

"That all sounds easy enough. Who else is going?"

"My friends from uni, and their wives or girlfriends. They're a fun crowd, you'll like them," he paused, "can I see you before that though?

I knew what he meant, but I wanted to be home as much as possible before James went away. "I have a really heavy week ahead, especially if I'm gonna get off early on Friday. How about a lunch date in your office?" I smiled and batted my lashes flirtily. Oscar grinned back.

"My office door has a lock."

"Hmm, what are you suggesting?" I pretended to look shocked. Oscar stroked my fingers across the table.

"Well if you wear a skirt and stockings to work tomorrow, you can find out." His touch left trails of heat running from my hands straight to my groin. I crossed my legs under the table. He smiled widely and winked like a naughty schoolboy. "Can you wear the heels too please," he whispered in his sultry voice.

"I'll see what I can do you dirty boy," I flirted, batting my lashes. It pleased me when Oscar came on strong. There were so many times that I felt unsure of him.

"You love it when I'm a dirty boy," he murmured.

"I sure do." With that, he lifted my hand to his mouth, and kissed the back of my hand softly. Everything south of my waist tightened.

The spell was broken when he glanced at his watch and told me that he had to be getting back. We made our way up, and sadly the lift was too packed for anything other than a peck goodbye when I reached my floor.

As I headed into my office, Lewis came out of his to find me. "Elle, need you in a meeting in two minutes. My office." I just had time to dump my handbag and trot down the corridor. When I opened the door, I was shocked to see two of the senior partners sitting with Lewis. After the hellos, Lewis asked me to sit.

"Mr Porenski has approached our firm to undertake a substantial amount of his legal work. Apparently his companies are now too big and complex, and the volume of work too much for his in house legal team, so he wishes to farm out the contract, and flotation work to a legal firm, and keep the legal work for mergers and acquisitions done in house. He has insisted that we meet a number of conditions, primarily concerned with his need for complete confidentiality. He requires a fixed team, including secretaries, all of whom must sign confidentiality agreements. He also requires Ms Reynolds to be his dedicated contact and co-ordinator at the company."

My hand flew up to my mouth. I had been flippant when suggesting Ivan become a client. I never in a million years had expected him to actually take me seriously. I could see the senior partners salivating at such a coup.

"This deal is worth a huge amount of both money, and prestige to the firm Miss Reynolds, as I'm sure you're aware," said Mr Carey, one of the senior partners, "how do you feel about becoming his point of contact? Are you comfortable with that?"

"What would be expected of me?" I wanted to know what sort of demands I was supposed to kowtow down to in order to keep him happy. From my perspective, I felt a strange mixture of professional pride that I'd instigated such a coup, and mortification because I felt Ivan was only doing this to get in my knickers.

"You would be expected to oversee the delivery of whatever services he needs us to provide. You would be directly responsible for all communications with him. He doesn't operate nine to five, so a level of flexibility would be required from you. We expect you to check everything is done on time, and to the standard he requires. We want no mistakes on this account. Are you up for this challenge?"

"Yes, I believe so. Has he indicated whether or not we're competing with other firms for this account?"

"No. He was quite clear. He came to us as he was impressed with you," said Lewis, "although I'm concerned about his motives."

"Hmm. I think you may be right there. I'm sure I can handle him. Has this all been agreed yet? Do we have a start date?"

"I have to call him to confirm that we can meet all his requirements, then we begin tomorrow. He insists that you have a private office, Elle, so we need to move you this afternoon. We also need to assign you a secretary, and get all the NDA's signed and sent up to Mr Porenski's office." Mr Carey smiled and stood up, "this is quite something of a coup for Pearson Hardwick, so we need to get on it. I'll show you your new office."

I followed Mr Carey out and down the corridor towards the executive offices. They were far swankier than the office I currently shared with Peter and the others, and were accessed via their own secretaries office. He pulled out a key and unlocked room 3. It had a roomy foyer area with a desk, computer and phone system for the secretary. In front of us was another door, which led into my new office.

The first thing I noticed was the view. Vast windows looked out over London, which shimmered slightly in the early summer heat. The office was large, furnished with a large desk, a seating area and bookshelves. It had thick, deep blue carpet, which muffled the sounds of the main secretarial area down the corridor. When Mr Carey closed the door, it was silent.

"Totally soundproofed, in case Mr Porenski asks," he said, "Lewis, can you re-assign all Ms Reynolds work, and assist her in getting this ready for tomorrow. You also need to assign her secretary and set her up in here. Maintenance can assist you with furnishings if these aren't to your liking." He handed me the key, and the two partners left.

Lewis looked at me, "I'll sort you a secretary, and get the NDA'S typed up. I thought Laura McIntyre might be a good choice. She's experienced and discreet."

I nodded, "yes, she'll be fine." I frowned, "Lewis, do you think I can do this?"

"Only one way to find out. I'm sure you'll be fine, and the rest of us are here as backup. This is a big deal for the firm, we won't let you fail."

"Thanks. This office looks very bare. I don't have lots of stuff to fill it. A few legal textbooks I suppose." I mused out loud as I wandered around the room. The other lawyers had full bookshelves and loads of personal stuff in their offices. I would have to go with a minimalist look. Lewis laughed.

"My shelves are overflowing, so I think some can be stored in here, and we can ask housekeeping for some plants and stuff. Come on, lets get this move done. I have a stack of work to get sorted." We headed back to grab my stuff.

It took less than an hour to re-assign my workload and move my things. I've never been one for tons of 'stuff' at work or anywhere else for that matter. I quite literally had pens, pencils and a calculator to move once my files had been farmed out to the others. IT came and set up my computer and email, and Lewis had the maintenance man move some of his books onto my shelves. The room still looked a bit bare, but I liked that. Less clutter meant I could think clearly.

A little while later, Lewis returned with Laura. She was one of the nicer secretaries, and was clearly delighted to have been picked for what was in effect a promotion. She stood in her new office, away from the gossip and bitching of the main floor, and sported the widest smile I'd ever seen.

"This is so cool. It's gonna be so much easier to work without all the noise and aggro. Has my computer been set up yet? Or do I need to call IT?"

"All done. They just left. You're good to go. Lewis, I just thought, Mr Porenski may want us to photocopy in private rather than in the copy room."

"Good point. Here are your NDA'S, I'll get these sent up, and then I'll sort the copier issue. Good thinking Elle." We signed the documents, and Lewis hurried away to pick up the ones signed by the partners and get them sent to Ivan, along with my contact numbers, fax number and office address.

I helped Laura move her things from her cubicle. Thankfully there wasn't much room on her desk there for tons of gonks, and fluffy pens, although I suspected that given half a chance, she'd fill her new office with sparkly crap. Even so, we moved two boxes of her personal stuff. Back in the office, she checked her computer. Satisfied that all was working ok, she began to unpack the photos, cutesy notebooks and glittery pens.

"Tea or coffee Elle, and do you have a favourite cup?" Laura looked at me expectantly. I had been lost in thought, staring at the magnificent view from my window.

"Coffee please. Milk no sugar thanks. I don't have a special cup." She hurried off. I dragged myself back to reality, and went in search of stationary.

Sitting in my new office sipping my coffee, Laura quizzed me on our new assignment. "I don't know yet what we'll be doing, it depends what Mr Porenski gives us. I know about as much as you right now, but I'm damn sure that'll change quick enough. He comes across as rather exacting."

"He comes across as rather gorgeous," she replied. We both laughed.

"This is a huge deal for the firm Laura, so no mooning over him or cows eyes. We have to really deliver on this." I was serious. Whatever Ivan's motives were, I had to remain professional, and make sure the company was represented properly. Men came and went, but I had to live with my career for the rest of my life.

We both jumped when my new phone rang. It was Ivan, his accent more pronounced on the telephone than normal.

"Good afternoon Elle, we are on the same side at last. I trust you now have a private office?"

"Hello Mr Porenski, I do indeed have a private office. Thank you for insisting on it."

"Call me Ivan please. We need to make a start. I have a few cases that I would like your company to handle, to test you out as it were. What time do you arrive in the morning?"

"7.30 normally. I can be earlier if you require."

"I'll meet you at Smollenskis for breakfast at eight. Bring a notepad."

With that, he rang off. I stared at the receiver for a few seconds, marvelling at the rudeness of the man.

Chapter 7

With no work to do, I left at five and raced home to see James. He was busy playing call of duty, but stopped when I walked in. "You're early? Did your boss take a kindness pill?"

"Nope. I start a new project tomorrow, and it's a biggie, so all my work was given to other people. I was twiddling my thumbs, after I moved into my swanky big office, that is," I grinned. I proceeded to tell James the story of my day, including every detail of my new secretary and posh private office.

"Well, if you tame this Ivan, you're definitely up for a pay rise or a promotion. Sounds like you earned your stripes faster than you expected. Just be careful of Oscar, he worries me, and by the sounds of it, this Ivan is very sweet on you."

"I'm not so sure. I'm now his lawyer, so we have to have a professional relationship. If he was 'sweet' on me, as you so charmingly put it, he would have kept away from me professionally, surely?"

James looked amused, "he was simply making sure that you weren't the opposing lawyer honey, that's when there would be a conflict of interest. Now, dinner. Shall we have chicken or prawn?

"Prawn please. Any more news from America?"

"Yup, they have recruited the team I'm to head up, I just have to ok them next week. There's way too much coding for one person on these apps, so I have to direct a whole group of geeky nerds. My idea of hell, but the money makes up for it." James busied himself chopping veg as I opened the bottle of Chardonnay I had picked up on my way home. I poured us each a glass, and sat watching James as he cooked.

"What does Oscar think of Ivan's actions?" James asked as he chopped the mushrooms. My hand flew to my mouth.

"I haven't told him yet. I never even thought of it."

James stopped and gave me a quizzical look, "but he's your boyfriend, right?"

"I don't know," I admitted, "we go out, we've done the nasty, and I think he likes me, but I don't know if it's exclusive. He might have other women for all I know. I might have other men. We haven't discussed it, although he asked if I was shagging you."

James looked pained. "Elle, you are better than that. You deserve a man who treats you like a goddess, not one that you can't say for sure if you're an item. Look in the mirror sometime."

"I know. I feel out of my depth with him, as if I'm not quite good enough, but I put that down to my own insecurities. You gotta remember that I'm surrounded every day by people who were born into privilege, and I'm often aware that I don't quite belong, regardless of how hard I work for it."

"You don't belong because you're better than them. To make it to a swanky office by sheer hard work alone is more than they could have done. Could they have made it to where you are if they hadn't had an enormous leg up in the first place?"

I thought about it, "no, probably not, but that doesn't make me any less of an outsider."

James raised his glass, "to the outsiders, and to quote Steve Jobs, to the square pegs in the round holes."

"I'll drink to that." We clinked glasses and both smiled. I noticed that James had the most perfect teeth. "James, can I ask you something?"

"Of course."

"What's with the beard and hair?" He looked uncomfortable, and I instantly regretted asking.

"My shield against the world."

"Oh?"

He sighed, "I used to take pride in how I looked, but it made no difference. Janine still left me. At least like this I don't have to think about women. In general they don't go for scruffy hairy blokes."

"So you're hiding behind it?"

"Yeah, I spose."

"Well, if it keeps you happy...." I trailed off.

"I'll shave it off one day, when I'm ready," he snapped, which made me flinch. "Sorry Elle, didn't mean to bite your head off."

"It's ok, I shouldn't have asked." I reached over and squeezed his hand, which he whipped away as if I'd burnt him. Embarrassed, I ignored it, and poured us each another glass of wine. James busied himself with the stir fry, and the awkwardness was buried.

After dinner, I decided on a long bath. Our favourite telly program didn't start till nine, so I spent a pleasant few hours exfoliating, shaving and body buttering in anticipation of my lunchtime assignation with Oscar the following day. When I was fully depilated and covered in body cream, James called out that our program was about to start. I threw on my dressing gown, and padded out to the lounge barefoot. James plonked a coffee down in front of me, and sat back to watch 'Mock the week'.

Just as the opening credits began, James yelped, "Elle, sleeve." I looked down to see a giant, hairy, spider sitting in the crook of my arm. I screamed, loudly, like a girl, and as panic gripped me, I dragged the robe off and threw it on the floor. James deftly whacked the spider with a magazine as it tried to crawl away.

It was at that moment that we both realised I was standing there starkers. Instinctively I tried to cover myself with my hands, feeling a deep blush rising up my cheeks. I had to let a hand uncover something in order to grab the robe. James just stood and stared.

"Turn round!" I barked at him. With a last rake of his eyes over me, he rather reluctantly swivelled around while I shook my robe before putting it back on, tying it tightly round my waist.

"Ok, I'm covered," I said, mortified. James turned back round sporting a deep blush, and I suspected, an erection.

"I'll get rid of the spider," he muttered, picking up the carcass and swiftly turning to run to his own bathroom. I heard the loo flush as he disposed of the body. It was at least five minutes before he returned, and we both settled to watch our programme with a slightly uneasy silence shimmering between us.

I was at Smollenskis by 7.45 the next morning, bright eyed, bushy tailed, and ready for Ivan, and whatever he wanted to throw at me. I was also ready for Oscar, wearing a skirt and stockings rather than tights. I found a table, and ordered a coffee.

Ivan was precisely on time, and flanked by two bodyguards. I wondered why he had wanted to meet in a restaurant rather than my private office when he had demanded I be given it. My breath caught as he approached my table, and I wondered whether seeing him frequently would lessen the effect of his beautiful face. He sat facing me, while his security took the table behind us. He smelt delicious, and looked as though he was fresh from a shower. It was too warm for a three piece suit, so he was wearing a dark blue two piece, a crisp white shirt, and a cerulean tie. The total effect was breathtaking.

He smiled widely as he shook my hand, "lovely to see you Elle. So much more civilised to meet over a meal I think. Now what would you like to eat?" I chose poached eggs on toast, and sat back as he ordered for both of us. Once the waitress had stopped batting her lashes at him and taken our order, he leaned forward, and whispered conspiratorially, "I just wanted to take you out for a meal."

I laughed, "isn't taking us on as your legal advisors a bit over the top to just have breakfast with me?" He smirked.

"I didn't think I'd get to have breakfast with you any other way, so yes, I hope it's totally worth it." His voice was seductive, almost purring. A voice made for phone sex. I pushed that unwelcome thought from my brain, and smiled brightly.

"So what have you got for me?"

"A contract of sale will be with you by two today. I need you to check it, and have it back to me by close of play at the very latest. Can you write down the terms I expect, if there are any anomalies, alert me immediately please." I pulled out my notepad and pen, and wrote quickly as he reeled off the terms he expected. He finished just before our food arrived, and I checked my notes as I ate, adding a few addendum's as I thought of them. I felt his eyes on me, and looked up to find him watching me intently as he ate his bacon and eggs.

"You're very exact," he said, "I like that. Explains why you have risen as quickly as you have."

"How much have you found out about me?" I asked, unsure whether I wanted to know the answer or not.

"Everything Elle. My people are exceptional at background checks. I know all there is to know about you."

"Oh." I blushed. My fear of exposure making my heart race. All the parts of myself which were buried deep had been brought into view. He knew where I was from. I looked down at the table, trying to will my blush away, and find the cool, calm, Elle-the-lawyer persona.

"I come from the slums of Moscow. Real slums, true poverty. Don't be ashamed of where you come from. I admire your achievements even more knowing you got there through talent and hard work. You're very impressive." He smiled tentatively.

"Have you told anyone else?" By that, I meant Oscar, but I didn't want to say it.

"Of course not. It's nobody else's business."

"Except yours?"

"Especially mine." He was back to that purring, seductive voice again. "I like to know the people I do business with Miss Reynolds, you can't blame me for that."

"Ok, I accept that, but I was rather it wasn't a subject for discussion. I worked hard to fit in, and I would rather my bosses didn't find out just how hard I had to work." I looked him straight in the eyes as I said it, and I figured that he understood. He nodded.

"I understand. Your secret's safe. You blend in well, apart from the fact that you stand out for other reasons."

"So do you. I would never have pegged you as starting out poor. You seem so urbane." I wanted to pay Ivan a complement, I wanted to keep him on side. I wanted to work well with him.

"We both know how much effort goes into our polished personas. So it appears we are kindred spirits Elle. Tell me, this weekend with Oscar, are you looking forward to it?"

I thought about it for a moment, "I don't really know. I've got no idea what to expect. I'm a bit nervous if I'm honest." Ivan nodded, and gave me one of his intense stares.

"You're very truthful. I like that. Listen, if you have any problems this weekend, I want you to call me. I'll be at my place."

"Thanks, but I don't anticipate there being any problems. This is a social weekend," I said, smiling. Ivan nodded to his bodyguard, who went and paid our bill.

"Any problems, I mean it. Oscar is a complicated man, and as a colleague now, you have my team at your disposal." With that cryptic remark, he stood up, and gave me a curt nod goodbye.

I ordered another coffee, and sat back to contemplate our meeting. It surprised me just how much I had liked Ivan. Once I'd got over his dazzling looks, he'd actually come across as a lot warmer than I'd expected. I went back over my notes as I finished my coffee, and headed up to my office.

Lewis pounced as soon as I walked in, "I've been looking for you. Any word from Mr Porenski yet?"

"Yes. I just had a breakfast meeting with him. We have a contract arriving at two to be checked. I have a list of his requirements to be ticked off against it, and he wants it back by five. No idea how long the contract will be though, so I may need assistance."

"Ok. Just let me know when it arrives."

"Will do. Anything I can help with this morning? I'm at a loose end till two."

"Laura can help in the filing room, you can help me with the Marsbury contract. I'll come to your office and we can zip through it together. It'll be good practice for this afternoon." Lewis went off to gather the paperwork, and I settled in my new office.

The morning sped by quickly, interrupted only by a text from Oscar.

midday my office?

To which I replied,

you bet xx

At five to twelve, I excused myself for lunch, and ducked into the ladies to remove my knickers, and tuck them into my handbag. Just walking through reception knickerless made me hyper aware of what I was about to do. The short journey in the lift was an exercise in anticipation, and I could feel myself getting slick and hot at the thought of what Oscar was going to do to me.

Glacial blonde gave me a blatantly hostile glare as I walked into reception. She strutted ahead of me as we made our way down the corridor to Oscars office, and scowled as she opened his door for me. Oscar smiled as I walked in, before raking his eyes down my body to rest on my high heels. In my knickerless state, I felt wanton and reckless. He dismissed her before striding over to lock the door. He wrapped his arms around me and kissed me hard, almost fucking my mouth with his tongue. His hands roamed over my back before sliding over my bum, and down my legs.

He toyed with the hem of my skirt for a few moments before edging it up to my thighs. As soon as he realised I wasn't wearing knickers, he groaned, and pulled my skirt up to my waist, standing back to look. "Dear god, you're going to kill me turning up like that."

I took a deep breath to steady myself. My arousal was coursing through me. "You like?"

"More than like, you look sensational. Please, on my desk." Oscars voice was hoarse, and he couldn't take his eyes off my exposed body. He pulled me over to his desk, and lifted me onto it, splaying my legs wide apart. His fingers lightly traced over the tops of my stockings, where silk met skin. His hands stroked down my leg, right down to my high heels. He swallowed noisily before lifting my foot to his face and running his tongue over the stiletto heel.

I watched, entranced, as he worshipped my high heels, kissing and licking them, while an impressive erection strained the front of his trousers. He spent at least five minutes in the adoration of my shoes, caressing and sucking each one in turn.

I was about to ask him to crack on, when he slid his hand up my leg and began to stroke my clit with the gentlest touch. He slipped a finger inside me, and I tightened around it, my insides beginning that delicious quivering that comes with extreme arousal. I began to pulse when he freed his throbbing erection.

He pulled a foil packet out of his pocket, and ripped it open with his teeth, rather than abandon my clit even for a moment. He slid it on and thrust inside me, lifting my feet to rest on his shoulders, and laying me back on his vast, mahogany desk. He moved inside me at a leisurely pace, pressing tiny circles on my clit with his thumb, while he continued to lick and kiss my shoes.

Seeing the pleasure on his face sent me rapidly over the edge. I came hard, the orgasm ripping through me like a firestorm. He moaned softly against my stiletto, moving his hands to grip both my thighs. Keeping his tongue on my shoes, he sped his thrusts before I felt him swell inside me, and come noisily. His body shuddered as he lost control, and he stilled for a moment, pressed into me, his brow furrowed in concentration.

He pulled out, and removed the condom, tying a knot in it before producing a tissue to clean me up. It was the most intimate act Oscar had ever done for me. He wrapped the condom in the tissue before tucking himself back into his trousers and righting his tie.

"Thank you for that," he said, before he went to his office bathroom to dispose of everything. I jumped off the desk and rummaged round in my handbag to find my knickers and restore myself to decency. Thankfully my skirt wasn't too wrinkled, and I was able to tidy my appearance, although the post orgasmic flush would take a few minutes to disappear.

"Have you got time to eat?" Oscar asked. I noticed there were two salvers set up on his table. I glanced at my watch, it was only 12.25.

"Yes. I've worked up quite an appetite," I said, smiling at him. We sat down, and he pulled the silver covers off the plates to reveal chicken salad. I took a sip of my wine, and looked up at him, "how am I going to be introduced at the weekend?"

"What do you mean?"

I took another sip, "are you introducing me as your friend, your girlfriend, or your bit of fluff?"

"Oh I see. My friend. If I introduce you to my mother as my girlfriend, she'll drive you mad with questions about your family tree, and heritage." He was matter of fact, and yet he'd just confirmed that what we had just shared was only as friends. My back went rigid, and I struggled to keep my face impassive. *Just a fuck buddy, not good enough to be his girlfriend,* my subconscious sneered. I took a deep breath and carried on eating. I decided to give Oscar's place a miss. My fragile ego couldn't take being anyone's dirty secret. I noticed that Oscar was watching my reaction.

"Is that a problem Elle?"

I didn't answer straightaway. The truth was that I really didn't know what to say that didn't include telling him to piss off. I finished eating, and wiped my mouth with the napkin.

"Yes, I think it's a problem if I'm honest. I want an open and honest relationship, not one where I'm introduced as a 'friend', as if I'm some sordid secret. I actually think I'm better than that." I stared at the cruet set, almost afraid to see his reaction.

"I see. How would you like to be described?"

I shrugged, "no idea, now if you'll excuse me, I need to be getting back." I picked up my bag, and turned towards the door, pausing only to unlock it. Behind me, I heard Oscar curse, but he didn't try and stop me. I didn't want to wait for the lift, so stomped down the stairs, getting angrier and angrier. I was cross with myself more so than Oscar. To be fair, he had promised me nothing, and owed me nothing. I had been more than willing to debauche myself on his desk, and I felt foolish for being upset. He clearly lived in a world with different rules than mine, and I needed to stop expecting him to behave like a normal person.

Chapter 8

Back in my office, I pulled myself together, and went over my notes from that morning, memorising them. At two sharp, the contract was delivered, and I started to go through it. Lewis arrived, and we decided to both go through it separately, as it wasn't particularly long, and I wanted to make sure I didn't miss anything. It turned out to be a contract of sale of an engineering company that Ivan was buying a controlling interest in. I logged on to companies house and purchased their last three years accounts, to reconcile the figures with the ones given in the contract.

Almost straightaway, I spotted a discrepancy in the directors loan accounts. The figures in the contract were vastly different from the ones lodged in their official accounts. When I pointed it out to Lewis, he borrowed my calculator and worked out the exact figures. It looked like the company was being used as the director's personal piggy banks.

This meant all the other figures were out, and the valuation was skewed. I called Ivan. "Hi Ivan, it's Elle, I spotted an issue with the directors loan accounts. The amounts lodged with companies house are 40% higher than they declared on this contract. Do you know if they have been paid back?"

"I wondered if you'd spot that," he purred, a smile in his voice, "no they haven't. What do you calculate the company to be worth now that you have uncovered it?"

"If you fire the board on takeover, just the 750k less than the offer price to reflect the higher loan account. If you keep the board, well, watch your back."

"Very good. Have you finished going through it?"

"No, not yet. Still a bit more for us to look at. I thought you wanted to know immediately we spotted anything?"

"Correct. While you're finishing, I will be renegotiating the price. Email me the figures I need as my negotiating point please before you get back to the rest of it."

"Will do."

He cut the call, and I sent over the companies house reports, as well as a scan of the figures in the contract of sale. Lewis was busy reading through the rest of it, referring to my notes as he went. He pointed out a potential issue with a lease on one of the factories, which, after a quick search on the land registry, proved to be near it's end, with the freehold owned personally by two of the directors, hiding behind a limited company.

"That lease will be up almost as soon as the company is sold. If Ivan fires the board, the rent could soar," Lewis pointed out. Immediately, I picked up the phone and relayed this to Ivan. He groaned.

"My legal team didn't pick that one up. Ok, I'll get on it, send me the details over please."

"Already have, plus the entry in the land registry."

"Thanks."

We didn't find anything else, but those two issues had made the company vastly overvalued. My phone rang. "The other party are meeting here at my offices, can you come up please?" Ivan said without preamble.

"On our way." I replied. Replacing the receiver, I turned to Lewis, "he has them coming over. We need to attend the meeting."

"This should be interesting," said Lewis, gathering up our papers. I had printed off the land registry and companies house reports, so we grabbed those, and made our way up to the fiftieth floor.

Ivan's office was a vast, modern space, full of sleek grey and taupe sofas, and dark wood. From the abstract art on the walls to the tasteful orchid displays, the place screamed restrained wealth. The receptionist was warm and friendly, showing us through to the conference room, and bringing us each a coffee. I organised our papers, and we waited. Ivan arrived first, flanked by the same two security guards from breakfast. They stood at the back of the room while he sat down next to Lewis.

"Given the information you have uncovered, I will be renegotiating the terms and price. If they refuse, I will be pulling out of the deal. The contract of sale may have to be rewritten quickly, as we all want this deal concluded today. Is that clear?"

"Yes. Not a problem," said Lewis, "we'll get it done."

The other directors arrived looking a bit cocky before Ivan dropped his first bombshell about the loan accounts. The finance director shifted uncomfortably in his chair before declaring the issue an 'oversight'.

"I see," said Ivan, "so tell me about Carridon property ltd, or was that an oversight too?"

The mood in the room plunged to sub zero. The two directors involved looked panicked, glancing nervously over at the two burly security men stationed near the door.

"It's not how it looks," said one of the directors, shooting a look over to one of the other men, "the price doesn't reflect the value of the freehold of that factory."

"So tell me sir," Ivan was sarcastic, "with a 750 thousand loan account, and no freehold, what exactly does the sale price buy me? An ailing company with a cash flow problem? About to be made worse by a rent increase on an ending lease? Come on gentlemen, what do you take me for?" They all squirmed in their seats, with the feeling of panic in the room almost palpable. Not only were they trying to take Ivan's money, they had attempted to bamboozle him too. Not a wise move on their parts.

Ivan took complete command of the room, the previously cocky men subdued and submissive. He declared his terms, and got them. He ended up paying the same price, but gaining the whole company and the freehold. I wished that I had been able to just watch him in a mesmerised admiration, but I had to concentrate on making copious notes to get the contract rewritten quickly.

We swept out of the room, flanked by security, and into Ivan's office to get the contract done ready for signing. Lewis and I sat at Ivan's computer, and I typed quickly, while we went through my notes. Lewis proofed as I typed. I glanced up to notice Ivan listening in an earpiece. He caught my eye, and grinned.

"Just hearing what they have to say now they are alone in the room," he said, before resuming his eavesdropping.

We got the contract done in record time, and printed off the copies required. Ivan's secretary delivered them to the conference room to allow the directors to read them in 'privacy' before we returned. Lewis and I sat and had a coffee while we waited, Ivan stood listening to the earpiece. After half an hour, Ivan's secretary indicated that they were ready for us, so we returned to the conference room. The board were sombre as they each signed the agreement, followed by Ivan. I couldn't help but notice that they all used expensive pens, while Ivan used an ordinary biro.

"Gentlemen, we are concluded here," said Ivan, "and as of now, your services are no longer required at the company. My security teams will accompany you back to the offices to remove your personal effects and change the locks. As per the contract of sale, there will be severance pay equal to statutory redundancy under the TUPE regulations. Good day gentlemen."

There was a stunned silence in the room. None of them could believe that Ivan would just fire the entire board that quickly. They had probably hoped that the duplicitous ones would be fired, and the rest would keep their cushy jobs. Ivan nodded to us, and we followed him out of the room and back to his office.

"Did they think you would only get rid of the ones who lied? Sacrifice three to save the other's jobs?" I asked, curious. Ivan grinned.

"Got it in one. They were all arguing amongst themselves in there, blaming the finance guy, and the two in the limited company. They all knew about it though, they had all been complicit."

He pulled out his mobile, and spoke quickly in Russian to someone, before cutting the call and turning to Lewis and I. "Ready for a drink? The two of you just saved me approximately what I'm going to be paying your company this year. I think you deserve champagne." He pressed his intercom, and jabbered something in Russian. A few moments later a flunky appeared with a trolley holding an ice bucket, a bottle of Krug, and three glasses. We toasted our success, and I took a long sip of the delicious drink.

"I like having you on my side, Elle," said Ivan, "I think this will be a profitable partnership."

"I hope so too," I said, glowing slightly with his praise. I drained my glass, and noting the time was nearly seven in the evening, said goodbye and left Lewis finishing his champagne.

James dished up a casserole as soon as I got home, and pushed a large glass of wine across the island to me. I sat on the bar stool and watched him, as he ladled out a delicious smelling beef stew onto large plates, followed by a heap of mashed potato he had stashed in the warming drawer. My mouth watered.

"You had a good day?" I asked.

"Yeah, just cleaned the flat really. Done a bit of the schematics for next week, got my clothes ready for packing, that kind of thing, you?"

I told him about my day, omitting my lunchtime assignation. I regaled him with an impression of Ivan terrifying a board of directors, doing my best impression of his heavy Russian accent.

"Serves them right for trying to pull a fast one," James said, "oh by the way, Oscar was looking for you, he knocked on the door earlier. Said he'd been trying to call you all afternoon." James pulled a face, and I was glad I hadn't told him about my knickerless escapade at lunch.

"I've had my mobile off. Anyway, I don't really want to speak to him. Apparently I'm only going as his 'friend' this weekend." I did air quotes with my fingers around the word friend. James scowled slightly.

"There really is something wrong with that man, he should be falling at your feet, not behaving as though he's ashamed of you. I don't blame you for not wanting to go. Staying at a castle is not exciting enough to compensate for being treated like that."

"Castle? How do you know he has a castle?"

"Google. His country seat is Conniscliffe castle. Don't you google people Elle?" James pulled open his laptop, and quickly typed one handed while he forked casserole into his mouth with the other hand. *Impressive James!*

"There you go," he said, turning the laptop to face me. It showed a picture of a beautiful castle, surrounded by formal gardens. I clicked onto the blurb, and read it had been built in

1265, had taken forty years to build, and had been in Oscar's family for three hundred years. It wasn't open to the public, was stuffed full of priceless art, and had two hundred rooms. Suddenly, I wanted to see it.

I pulled my mobile out of my handbag and saw straightaway that I had ten missed calls from Oscar. I opened the text from him.
sorry I upset you. Please don't ignore me. Call me Oxxx

I placed my phone on the counter, and went back to my dinner. James was staring at me.

"Did something happen with him today?"

"We had lunch." I wasn't going to share more than that, so I changed the subject. "What's on the agenda tonight?"

"Well, it's shit on the telly. Fancy a film? I have maltesers."

I laughed, "you really know how to tempt a girl." James waggled his eyebrows, and grinned. I cleared up and made coffee while James scrolled through the film menu, calling out suggestions. We settled on 'Avatar', which neither of us had seen. I flopped onto the sofa, and stuffed a pillow under my head, while James shared the chocolate between two bowls, plonking mine down in front of me.

Shortly after the film began, my mobile rang. Seeing it was Oscar, I ignored it, and switched my phone off, praying he wouldn't come up and knock on the door.

James' presence must have put him off, as he didn't bother me for the rest of the evening. I must have fallen asleep, as the next thing I was aware of was James picking me up, and carrying me gently to my room. I was barely aware as he laid me down on my bed, removed my high heels, and covered me with the duvet before softly kissing my forehead, and tiptoeing out.

I awoke the next morning with my skirt round my waist and my blouse twisted and digging into my armpit. Realising I was still fully dressed, I quickly stripped off, and changed into my gym gear. I headed into the kitchen to make tea. James was already there, looking bleary.

"You were out cold last night. I hope you didn't mind me putting you to bed," he said.

"Thank you. I would still be on the sofa otherwise. It must have been the wine, champagne and tension knocked me out." We sipped our tea in companionable silence. "I'll try and get home earlier tonight so we can have a proper evening before you leave."

"Great. I'll do a roast," he replied. I quickly sorted my gym bag, and headed off to the gym.

I was right at the end of my workout when Oscar walked in. I'd never seen him there early before, as he had made it plain he wasn't an early riser. He strolled over to the treadmill I was on and stood right in front of me. I slowed it to a stop, and took a swig of water.

"Hi Oscar, what can I do for you?" I asked in a sarcastically sweet voice.

"Didn't that flatmate of yours give you my message last night?" He asked with his usual scowl.

"Oh yes, James told me you dropped by. I fell asleep after dinner, hope you understand, but I was exhausted last night." I smiled.

"I see. So you're not ignoring me then?"

"No. Why would I do that?"

Oscar leaned towards me, and whispered in my ear, "because I'm an ass, and because I fucked you, then in the same hour basically told you that you were just a friend. Terribly bad manners I know, I just hope you can forgive me." His warm breath caressed my ear, sending a little shiver down my spine. I looked into his eyes, trying to read his emotions. He looked contrite, and a little sad.

"Of course, really don't worry about it. In actual fact it answered my question as to whether or not you expected exclusivity." I stopped to let the statement sink in, and smiled brightly as he scowled some more.

"Has Ivan asked you out?" He snapped. I did my best to look affronted.

"No, I'm his lawyer, not his girlfriend. It's strictly business with Ivan. I'm surprised you think anything different."

"Hmm. Who then?"

"That's none of your business Oscar. I don't ask who you're seeing."

"For gods sake Elle, I'm not seeing anyone else. I seem to spend half my time chasing around after you."

"Do you normally chase after your friends?" I asked before I sauntered over to the changing room. I heard him curse as I walked into the safety of the ladies showers. *Elle 1, Oscar 0*

I made it into my office by 7.45, and immediately checked my emails to find one from Ivan requesting an early meeting at eight in the same place we had breakfast the day before. I let Lewis know, before hot footing it down in the lift. I got there about a minute before Ivan, who immediately ordered coffees. As soon as we had chosen our breakfasts, Ivan got to the point of the meeting. He had placed an interim manager in the engineering company, so needed a contracts for him drawn up, plus all the TUPE rules for the employees had to be followed, so their old contracts needed checking, rewriting for the new company, and new HR systems introduced.

"I don't want my legal team bogged down with it, there are over a thousand employees. It's basic employment contracts that interns can draw up, and I need it done fast."

"Ok. Let me talk to the managing partner and find out how many trainees I can have, so I'll sort that first thing. Does your team have standard employment contracts they use? I'll need a copy. Same for the interim. I'll need access to the HR records for the staff." I made copious notes as I talked.

"I have some bad news," said Ivan, making me stop and look up.

"Oh?"

"The current system is paper based only. It's a complete mess. Some records are incomplete, some are inaccurate, and I suspect some have been faked."

"You're joking, right? A thousand staff, and a manual system?"

"Yes, the interim manager practically laid an egg. My IT teams are in there today setting up a computerised system, the one all my companies use, but the information needs to be verified before its inputted."

"Ok, where is this company?"

"Sussex, not far from my home. I can put you and your team in a hotel, or you can stay at my house, I'm not there during the week."

"Ok, leave it with me, and I'll see what I can organise. It won't be cheap though, putting a legal team in a hotel for a week or two to get this done."

"Paying fake staff will cost more in the long term, so it's not an issue. I'll let you consult with your superiors, and see what Pearson Hardwick can rustle up.

"Ok. How many staff are you authorising the expenses for on this? Also how much room will we have to operate? It's no good taking loads of trainees there if they're all squeezed into one office."

"I'll commit two hundred thousand to this, and there is loads of room since I kicked out all the useless leeches. I won't be putting computers in every room, but there will be space for fifteen."

I took a deep breath. "Leave this with me. I'll call you mid morning, and if we're in agreement, we can begin tomorrow. I'll have to check how to get there by train, so could you include the address in your email please."

Ivan looked incredulous, "don't you drive?"

"No. I don't need to. I live round the corner." I blushed slightly.

"A car and driver will be put at your disposal. I would prefer you to have some security, so this will serve two purposes." Ivan said with a serious look on his face.

"I don't need security," I spluttered, "and I certainly don't need a full time driver."

"No arguments. You are going into a hostile takeover as my representative. You need protection, and you certainly need transport down there, rural Sussex isn't well served by public transport."

I rubbed my hand over my face, thinking about the enormity of the task ahead, and the potential problems I would face. "How were they paying employees without a computer system?"

"All done in ledgers, like something out of the dark ages. Monthly cheques issued, signed individually by hand." Ivan smiled, "can you imagine doing that every month? I have fifty odd thousand employees, I'd do nothing but sign cheques."

"Your biro would run dry," I sniggered. He laughed, a deep, hearty laugh at the absurdity of the idea. "I need to get back and crack on," I said, " I have a lot to organise."

Chapter 9

Back at the office, I went straight to Lewis and outlined the task. His eyes widened as I told him the budget. "Wow, he's not messing about. Let me get Mr Carey in."

Within minutes, the senior partner arrived, and sat as I outlined the task again. He contacted the city office, and spoke briefly with Ms Pearson, before addressing Lewis and I, "ok, 15 trainees are being sent over here this afternoon to be briefed. I suggest we also include several secretaries to assist with typing, data input and filing. Elle, you will be managing this case, with Lewis providing consultation as required. All staff requirements have been approved by Ms Pearson already, so if you need more once you get there, just speak to Lewis. Your PA will need to organise travel warrants and accommodation for everyone. Any resources you need Elle, we will provide."

"Thank you sir, I'll liaise with Mr Porenski's staff this morning and get up to speed on their HR system and processes, and get copies of their standard employment contracts. I'll spend the afternoon with the trainees, and brief them on the task. Mr Porenski is providing me with a car and driver, so I'll get down to Sussex early tomorrow morning to see what is there, what space we have, and decide how I'll organise it."

"Ok Elle, don't forget, whatever you need, just ask. Now lets get this done," said Lewis, banging his fist on the desk, which made Mr Carey jump.

Back in my office, I set Laura to work on the transport and accommodation requirements, while I called Ivan. "Hi Ivan. All systems go here. I have 15 legals and five support staff organised. I'll be briefing them this afternoon, so I need to speak to your head of HR to find out your protocols, and some sample copies of your employment contracts please."

"Fantastic. I'll have Mr Ranenkiov call you to organise all that for you. He is my director of human resources. When will you be starting?

"First thing tomorrow morning, if that's ok? Will your driver be able to pick me up early? I want to get there before the team to get the offices ready."

With the driver booked, I waited in my office for the call from Ivan's HR man. I didn't have to wait long. He arranged to come down to my office after emailing me the documents I'd need. Laura printed them off in between phone calls to hotels and the company we purchased travel warrants from.

Mr Ranenkiov was younger than I expected, with fair hair, strikingly pale blue eyes, and the squarest jaw I'd seen outside of a fashion magazine. His voice was less heavily accented than Ivan's, and his English just as impeccable. He shook my hand warmly, and accepted a cup of tea from Laura as we sat down.

We spent a fairly pleasant hour running through the procedures he wanted performed, the information he wanted collecting, and the way the data should be inputted. Each employee would be interviewed, identity verified, handbook issued, new contract drawn up and signed, everything cross checked against the paper records, and then inputted along with salary details in the new computer system. I took copious notes, referring to the documents he had sent, which, to be honest, walked us through the procedure.

"Their systems are non existent. It's a mess there. I don't envy you this task," he said, "there's a mad old woman in charge of it all right now, who guards it like a Rottweiler, and won't take kindly to computerisation."

"She won't get a say in it. If needs be, I'll begin a capability hearing with her. Mr Porenski can't run a company using ledgers and quills."

"Correct. I bet Mr Control Freak threw a fit when he saw it."

"Mr Control Freak?"

"Ivan is the ultimate control freak. Please don't tell me you haven't noticed?" He laughed, "I bet he's arranged a bodyguard for you already. He'll be reviewing your home security and doing a background check on your boyfriend next."

I laughed, "I think he's already done all that. It doesn't bother me, I quite like it."

We finished our meeting by half eleven. I sat at my desk reading through the documents, making further notes as I went. I was interrupted just before 12 by Laura, announcing the arrival of Lord Golding. Oscar strode into my office looking sheepish. He plonked himself down in the chair opposite me, and waited for Laura to leave.

"Hello again Lord Golding, to what do I have this pleasure twice in one day?" I asked. He smirked when I called him Lord Golding.

"Thought I'd take you to lunch while I grovel," he said, "I owe you an explanation, and I don't want to lose you."

"But I'm just your *friend* Oscar, you don't need to grovel for just telling me the truth."

"Come, let's go eat, and we need to talk."

We went down to the arcade, and Oscar led me to a small Italian restaurant on the ground floor. It was cosy and intimate, and smelt wonderful. We ordered our food, and made small talk until the waiter had poured our wine. When we were alone, Oscar grabbed my hand across the table, and held it firmly.

"I don't really know how to deal with this," he began, "there's so much I need to say to you, but I seem to excel in upsetting you."

"Ok, how about this, I won't speak for five minutes, I'll just listen."

Oscar took a deep breath, and seemed to compose himself. "My life is spent in the company of people to whom titles and stature are terribly important, you know, which family you're from, that sort of thing. I'm expected to marry a Rothchild, or similar, produce children, and carry it all on. It's accepted that I may not have feelings for the woman I marry, so it's quite normal to have a mistress as well. I've put off getting married for as long as possible, but my mother is beginning to put pressure on me. I knew if I took you home as my girlfriend, given that you don't have a title, she'd freak out, and try and make me see 'sense'. Plus my old Bullingdon pals will be there with their 'honourable lady' girlfriends. I thought if I introduced you as my friend, they would all be more inclined to be warm and welcoming." He scanned my face for a reaction. "You see, there's something about you, and I can't leave you alone. I know every man in the tower, including Ivan is salivating over you, and quite frankly I don't care that you're not titled."

He slumped back in his seat, watching my face for a reaction. I thought about what he'd said. "Oscar, how would feel if I took you to meet my friends, and was so ashamed of you, I introduced you as a friend? I felt like a fuck-buddy, and it's not a feeling I'm acquainted with, and I don't like it. I can't help where I came from, only where I'm going."

"I admire you for that," said Oscar, "to rise up despite no head start, it takes guts. The thing I can't fathom out about you is that you don't seem to care if you never see me again, most women are devastated if I leave them. You seem so self contained, and unimpressed. When you called me Lord Golding back there, it almost sounded like an insult."

"It was," I said flatly. "Titles hold no fascination for me. I told you that already. Like I said, none of us have a choice where we're born."

He stared at the cruet set, "I know. I feel like such a bastard for making you think you were, how did you put it? A fuck-buddy. I would never ever treat you like that Elle, you are far more to me than that."

I softened slightly. "So what am I to you?"

He swallowed, "here, you are my girlfriend, the one I take out, spend time with, care about. At Conniscliffe? I'm not sure, my lover perhaps? I just know how vile my mother was to the last girl I took there, and I don't want to put you through it. Snobbery can be difficult to handle at the best of times."

"I thought titles went through the male line? So it shouldn't matter one way or another for females." I asked.

"I agree. Sadly, my mother is a crashing snob, and thinks that nobody is good enough for her precious boy unless they are a princess, lady, or viscountess. Preferably with their own private bank in the family too. It kind of narrows the field somewhat."

"Yes, I can see it would be a problem. Doesn't your mum ever worry about inbreeding?"

Oscar snorted, "I doubt it's ever crossed her mind, even though there are lots of birth defects in our circles, they don't seem to put two and two together. More worried about keeping the fortunes in their families I suppose. Trust you to think about the practical aspects."

I smiled, "always practical."

"So am I forgiven Elle? I know I'm rubbish at the romance thing, and a crap boyfriend, but if you can allow me some room to screw up, I'll do my best to be a better one." He gave me a hopeful smile, and sipped his wine nervously.

"Ok. Forgiven, but not forgotten," I said. He relaxed back in his chair.

"So will you still come this weekend?

"Sure. I'll be down in Sussex working tomorrow, so I can get my driver to drop me at yours when I finish. It'll save me coming back to London.

"Driver? How come?" He frowned.

"I'm working on a huge project at the firm Ivan just bought. Leading a team of fifteen of Pearson Hardwick's finest. Ivan lent me a car and driver for the duration."

"I see, well it's no bother to pick you up. I'll be there around five. Text me the address."

We spent the rest of our meal discussing the functions Oscar had coming up. I didn't volunteer to accompany him, as I didn't possess any dresses suitable, and had spent my clothes fund for the month. There was no way I was admitting that one though.

I headed back to my office at one to hold a meeting with the trainees, and brief them on the work they were expected to do. As I anticipated, the majority were excited at the prospect of a week out of London, but a couple of the girls grumbled about having to be away from home. I narrowed my eyes, and reminded them that this was a prestigious account, and a real coup for the firm. I chose not to let on that I wouldn't be staying at the Travelodge with them, but at a billionaire's country pad.

When they were all fully briefed, I handed out the travel warrants, and the travel directions, and let them go home, with strict instructions to be at the factory by nine am the next morning. When they had all gone, I went back to my office to check over my notes again. Lewis stuck his head round my door and asked for a word.

"This is a bit of a delicate matter Elle," he said, shifting uncomfortably in his chair.

"Spit it out Lewis."

"Last night, after you left, well, Ivan asked if the company had any problem if he asked you for a date." Lewis went a bit pink.

"I see. What did you tell him?"

"I said it was none of our business. As long as you do nothing illegal or immoral, what you do in private is up to you. I do think he came to our company to get closer to you in the first place, so I wasn't entirely surprised."

"Thanks for telling me. I appreciate it." I said warmly. Lewis seemed to relax in front of me.

"Be careful Elle, he's a powerful man."

"I know. I'll be careful, I promise. Now would you mind if I finished at five today? I have stuff to get ready at home."

"Course not. Take the rest of the afternoon if you want."

I didn't need telling twice. Within fifteen minutes I was packed up, and on my way home, stopping only to buy a couple of bottles of chilled white wine.

"Is something wrong?" James asked, when I arrived home at half three.

"Nope, just skipped off early. I need to pack, I'm working away next week too, and away this weekend now, so I need to get ready for both."

"Made up with Oscar then?"

"Yep. He grovelled."

"Good. Where are you going next week?"

"A project involving an engineering company with outdated employment contracts in Sussex. I'm heading a team of trainees to go and sort it, so I'll be staying down there."

"That'll keep you out of mischief for the week. I'll be leaving at nine tomorrow morning, so I'll close up the flat properly if you won't be back here for a while. You know, empty the fridge and stuff."

"Great thanks." I dumped the wine bottles in the fridge, and headed to my room to pack. I decided on a weekend bag, and a separate case for my work clothes for the week. I was pleased that I wouldn't be lugging it all on the train. With my laptop and the papers I had to take with me, it would have been quite a feat. My wardrobe looked decidedly depleted, and I made a mental note to up my clothing budget as soon as possible.

True to his word, James had prepared a roast chicken with all the trimmings. The pair of us quickly demolished the first bottle of wine, and started on the second. We both ended up having a decidedly giggly and fun evening. James regaled me with funny stories from his travelling, and I made him laugh with my tale of the first time I got drunk at uni, and woke up in a wheelie bin.

"I'm thinking of shaving my beard off," announced James suddenly.

"Oh go on, it'll be too hot in California. Can I watch?" We both giggled.

"No," he said primly "when I get there, and I don't know anyone, I might try it. If I feel naked, it will have grown back by the time I get home."

"We'll you've seen me naked, I think I should see you." I blushed at the memory of spidergate.

"True. You have great tits by the way. I even saw the nips and everything," James teased.

"That's mean. I was being attacked by a giant spider! You weren't meant to be looking." I pouted, "anyway, showing your chin isn't the same as showing your naughty parts."

"That's a good point. I might try a goatee though," I pulled a face, "or maybe not." James quickly added after seeing my reaction.

"If that beard comes off, then I want a photo emailed to me. I've often wondered what you look like."

"Really?" James seemed pleased.

"Well I've only seen your eyes and teeth. Unless you have pre-beard photos I can see?"

"Nope. No photos. Sorry. I got rid of them when Janine went."

I didn't know what to say to that, so changed the subject. "Any nice ladies working with you out there?"

"No, all spotty, slightly greasy nerds. Coding isn't the type of job that attracts the glamorous women. It's better that way, as it's easier to concentrate, especially for the hormonal teenagers. If you walked in, they would all combust in a heap."

I giggled, "I'm hardly Kate Moss, James, but I get your point. A couple of months spent with horrid boys who squeeze their spots in the washrooms will at least make you glad to be over thirty."

"Very true, especially when they film themselves spot popping, and post it up on YouTube." James scrubbed at his face, "and I'm gonna be in charge of the little scrotes. What have I let myself in for? I could stay here and quietly code games, no bother to anyone. Why did I say yes to this?"

"I believe it was the quarter of a million quid they offered you."

"Oh yeah. Two months though..."

"Two months is nothing James. It'll take me years to earn that. You'll be back by July."

"Do you fancy a holiday when I get back? Somewhere hot, where we can just flop around on a beach, read books and drink cocktails?"

It took me by surprise. I hadn't been on holiday in years, partly because of work, and partly because I was scrabbling to pay off my student loans. The idea was enticing, and the two of us got along well. "That's a great idea. Where do you fancy going?"

"I don't mind, the med, Greece, anywhere, I'm not fussed. Shall we say last two weeks of July for work purposes, and I'll organise something while I'm away. It'll give me something to do. Just let me know when you have booked the dates off at work." James grinned.

"It's a deal," I said, "I'm looking forward to it already." I grinned back.

The rest of the evening seemed to pass by in a flash, and all too soon it was time for bed. I knew I had a heavy day ahead, so set my alarm for half five.

Chapter 10

I awoke just before the alarm, and headed into the kitchen area to make tea. There was no sign of James, so I decided to wake him up if he wasn't up by six. I quickly showered and washed my hair before pouring more tea to drink while I did my makeup. I dressed in the navy dress and jacket, and knocked on James' door.

"It's alright, I'm awake," he yelled. I quickly made him a fresh tea, and went back to my room to put my shoes on, and gather my luggage. When I dragged it all to the front door, James had appeared in the kitchen.

"I'm gonna head down, my driver should be here at six," I said, checking to make sure I had my keys and phone. James bounded over, and surprised me by enveloping me in a bear hug.

"I'm gonna miss you. Promise me you'll be careful?" He said.

"I'll miss you too. Text, email and call me yeah?"

"Will do." With that, he gave me a bristly peck on the cheek, and released me. He held the door as I lugged my case, bags, and laptop to the lift, and stood watching as the doors slid shut.

My driver was waiting outside, and immediately took charge of my case and bags, loading them carefully in the boot. He introduced himself as Roger, before holding the door open for me. I slid into the luxurious Mercedes, and checked my mobile. No messages was a good thing, and I sank back into the soft leather seats, and asked Roger to put the radio on.

The journey down to Sussex took nearly two hours, so I was glad I left home as early as I did. Roger had the keys to access the car park, which was deserted, and the offices. I found a door marked 'HR', and walked into chaos. There were files stacked almost floor to ceiling, on rickety shelves, with papers hanging out of most of them. There were papers strewn over every available surface, with boxes full of papers all over the floor. On the desk was an old fashioned typewriter, with a sleek new desktop shoved to the side. I suspected that the desktop had been installed the day before, and had been regarded as a waste of desk space.

I found ten empty offices on the ground floor, all of which must have been quite plush, but had marks on the walls where pictures had been removed, and dust everywhere. I headed up to the first floor, and found the remaining five rooms that had been fitted with computers for us. I checked that IT had provided each room with company handbooks, paper, staplers and pens as I had requested, and headed back downstairs. Roger stood unobtrusively in the corridor.

As the trainees appeared, I assigned each one to a room, and asked them to wait. By nine, my entire team were in and at their desks. The HR lady turned up at quarter past nine. She was a bumbling, grey haired woman in her early sixties, who seemed blissfully unaware of how appalling her systems had been.

"I'd like to introduce myself, I'm Elle Reynolds, Mr Porenski's lawyer." I said holding my hand out. She shook it nervously.

"Marion Smith, pleased to meet you. Can I ask why you're here?"

"I have the task of computerising all your staff records, and issuing the new employment contracts under the TUPE rules." I smiled my friendly smile to disarm her.

"We don't need computerising. I manage quite well thank you," she huffed, "and I'll get around to the new contracts in my own good time."

"Mrs Smith, Mr Porenski doesn't share that point of view, so I would appreciate your assistance to get this task done as quickly and easily as possible, so we can get out of your way. Now, first of all, I need an up to date list of employees who are on today's shift please."

"Oh, I don't keep shift records. The foreman does that," she said.

"Ok, I'll find the foreman. We will be processing every employee, and will need the relevant files and records as we go. I will assign you an assistant to help you retrieve the paperwork that we need." I hurried down to the factory floor, and eventually located the foreman, whose name was Jim. He agreed to send up fifteen staff at a time, and gave me a list of the full shift. I gathered the support secretaries and tasked them with finding the files for three people each. It was then that we discovered that everyone had been filed under their first names. Marion sat watching, looking amused.

"I know where every record is in that lot," she said proudly.

"Then would you get off your arse and give us a hand please?" I snapped.

"No need to speak to me that way young lady. I'll have you know I've been working here longer than you've been alive. Now I don't need a new system, so I suggest you take your fancy secretaries and head back to London. You're not welcome here. We're fine as we are."

"You were about to go bust as you were," I said, "your company has been sold, and with that comes a new boss. This is how he wants things done, and it's not up for discussion or debate." I kept my voice low and controlled. The rancid old cow just sat there and ignored me, before putting a sheet of paper in the decrepit old typewriter and pounding the keys. I fervently hoped she was typing out her resignation letter.

We found the first fifteen files, and delivered them to each lawyer, along with the corresponding members of staff. That then gave us another half hour to search the shelves for the next fifteen. It was going to be a long day.

As none of the staff had ID on them, they would all have to provide them on Monday, meaning we were working less efficiently. I went and found Jim and asked if he had a list of emails, or even phone numbers for the workforce.

"Only in my phone," he said, frowning, "I could text them all, but texts are expensive, and I only get 500 free ones."

"1000 texts will cost what? £100? I can give you that from petty cash if you would do that for me."

"In advance though."

"Fine." I rifled through my bag, and pulled £100 out of the contingency fund that Lewis had given me the previous day. Jim counted it before tucking it into his pocket, and pulling out his phone. He found the text screen and handed it to me to type a message. I just put that everyone needed to bring two forms of ID and their bank details with them on every shift next week until they have been enrolled on the new system. He pressed send, and I breathed a sigh of relief.

The system we created meant that each legal would be responsible for holding the files for each employee they interviewed and entered on the system. That way, any missing paperwork would be easier to track and sort. What we weren't prepared for was the complete absence of salary details in the employee records. Those were kept in huge ledgers, which would have to be checked to find the individuals rate of pay. I decided to get the interim manager to do that from Marion's computer, as she wasn't using it. It was either that or running between fifteen offices with the ledgers. He grumbled a bit, but got on with it.

I had set a target of processing 150 staff a day. The trainees worked like Trojans, only stopping briefly to scoff the sandwiches I had delivered. Laura made a start on the boxes of papers, despite Marion's protestations. They turned out to house papers that should have been filed, some from years back.

"This is a disgrace," muttered Laura as she efficiently put everything in alphabetical order.

"I heard that, cheeky moo," shouted Marion. I peered over her shoulder while she was glaring at Laura to take a peek at what she'd been typing. The fucking church newsletter!! She was watching us slog with her stupid filing system, while typing up her voluntary work on the firm's time and stationary. I grabbed the paper out of the typewriter.

"A word please," I said to the interim manager. We went to a side office where I showed him the offending document.

"I'll deal with her. Would you witness please?" He said.

I set my iPhone to record, and invited her into the room. The interim manager told her that due to her misuse of company property, doing personal business in company time, and her refusal to assist my team with a task that fell within her job description, she would face a disciplinary hearing next week. He told her she could have a colleague or trade union representative with her, and asked her to concentrate on the tasks she was given to do. She promptly went back to her desk and started crying. The manager escaped to type his letter, leaving me to deal with her.

"Listen, why don't you take a tea break, compose yourself?" I suggested.

"You just want to get rid of me," she howled, spraying spittle and snot over her already rusty typewriter.

"No, I just want you to do the job that you're paid to do," I said coldly. "Marion, the law says that these contracts must be done. I don't make the law, I just administer it. Mr Porenski has fifty thousand employees, he can't do payroll by hand. He needs this done and correct before the end of the month, otherwise people won't be paid on time, and that's not fair on them."

She stopped crying, and sniffed. "I don't know how to use a computer."

"That's what we're here for. When we get this under control, I'll teach you how to switch it on and do the things you need to do. It's not as complicated as those ledgers. I need to get it under control first though."

"Ok, I'll help."

With Marion's assistance, we began to motor. In between finding files, she helped the interim guy find the entries for each person in the ledger, and he showed her how to pull up an employee file, and enter the pay amount. I managed to find a moment to text the address to Oscar, and brush down my dusty dress. I called Ivan to let him know we were getting on top, and everything was going smoothly. I also called Lewis, as I knew he'd be like a cat on a hot tin roof until I reassured him that everything was progressing as planned.

We completed our 150 target by four, and even managed to squeeze in a few extras. By 4.30, I congratulated the team, and sent them home for the weekend. I went into the ladies and retouched my makeup before collecting my weekend bag from Roger, sending him home, and heading out into the fresh air to meet Oscar.

He stepped out of a black range rover, and took my bag before opening the passenger door for me. "Hard day?"

"Just a bit. I feel like I've been run over by a steamroller. I wanted to look my best to meet your friends, and instead I'm covered in dust."

He brushed some dust off my shoulder before kissing me quickly. "That bad?"

"Yup. Paper everywhere, a mad old bat who cried and sprayed me with snot, and about forty years worth of dust. I need a drink. How was your day?"

"Well my office was nice and clean. Had a lunch with another bank chairman, and signed a couple of things, so not terribly taxing."

I didn't reply, preferring to watch Oscar drive. He drove confidently through the winding lanes, his soft hands caressing the leather steering wheel. He seemed to relax in front of my eyes.

"Do you prefer Sussex to London?" I asked.

"Oh yes. I love the countryside. I feel like a fish out of water in the city sometimes," he said without hesitation. "I grew up here, lived here until I went to university. Well, in the school holidays that is."

"I would never have pegged you as a country boy. You seem very urbane."

"Sometimes people aren't everything they seem at first glance. You should know that..." I was just about to get upset, when he went on, "what with being a lawyer."

"Hmm." I said, looking out of the window at the beautiful countryside.

About ten minutes later we pulled up at a pair of enormous, wrought iron gates. Oscar tapped a code into a keypad by the side of them, and slowly they swung open. He drove on, down a long, winding driveway, flanked by trees. It seemed to go on for ages. Eventually, the trees stopped, and the road widened to give me my first view of Conniscliffe Castle.

"It's beautiful," I gasped, as it loomed up above us, perched on top of a hill.

"Thank you. Glad you approve."

Oscar pulled up outside an ornate entrance. The huge, doors swung open, and a uniformed man appeared. He opened my door, and proceeded to take my weekend bag from the back seat. I hopped out of the car, and followed Oscar into the castle. The entrance hall alone took my breath away. It was completely panelled in intricately carved mahogany, with a majestic sweeping staircase dominating the centre. It was carpeted in thick, deep red, and every piece of furniture looked like it was a priceless antique.

I'd expected it to smell like a musty old castle, like the ones I'd visited on school trips as a child. The only smell was furniture polish, and perfume from the large arrangement of flowers on a scalloped mahogany side table.

"The others are already here sir. They are in the drawing room with your mother."

"Thank you Jones. Elle, what would you like to drink?"

"I would love a glass of wine if that's ok." Oscar took my hand and led me down a wide corridor towards where I could hear voices.

"Call my mother Lady Golding." Oscar whispered before we walked in. I smiled up at him gratefully. It would never have occurred to me to ask him how to address her. I plastered my professional smile on as we walked through the ornately carved door into the vast drawing room. There were about ten people sitting on the various sofas and damask covered chairs. They all looked up as we entered.

"Hello everyone, glad you all made it ok." Oscar smiled at everyone, "I'd like to introduce my close friend, and lover, Elle Reynolds." He took me round the room, introducing me to all the hooray Henrys and Henriettas, before I came face to face with his mother.

"Mother, this is Elle, Elle, this is my Mother."

"I'm delighted to meet you Lady Golding," I said, shaking her proffered hand. She smiled graciously, but the smile didn't reach her eyes.

"Such a pretty girl Oscar, I can see why you like her. Tell me Elle, is that your natural hair colour?"
What? Is this woman rude or nuts? What a thing to ask!

"Oh yes, completely natural."

"How fascinating. It looks dyed."

"No, I'm fortunate that I don't need to colour it yet. No grey hairs." I looked pointedly at her dyed brown hair, with a touch of grey root peeking out at her hairline." She glared at me.

"Oscar tells me that you have to work for a living. It's odd how he has a fascination for working class girls ever since rehab and that terrible addiction problem." *What addiction problem? What a bitch.*

"I'm a corporate lawyer, that's hardly considered working class Lady Golding." I almost spat out the 'lady' prefix. She was anything but.

"Oh wow, that is so hard to get into!" an enthusiastic voice squealed. Bunty/Minty or whatever her name was, must have taken pity on me. "The training takes absolutely yonks, doesn't it Elle?"

"Took me about six years."

"Come and sit next to me and tell me all about it," she said, patting the seat next to her. "One of Harvey's friends did it. Said it was really tough to get into. Harvey's my brother by the way." She smiled a genuine smile, and I let out the breath I'd been holding. Oscar sat next to me, and firmly grasped my hand, despite the death stare his mother shot him. At that moment, I felt sorry for him. His mother was probably the coldest person I'd ever met, and I felt a lesser woman than I would have run from the room within the first two minutes. I flexed my steel backbone, and put my impassive face on, concentrating on the conversations going on around me. I heard Oscar call the girl next to me Minty.

"So did you have to go to uni?" Asked Minty

"Yes, I went to Cambridge. Did you go to uni?"

"Edinburgh, did art history. Pretty pointless but made some nice friends."

"Do you work?"

"Oh no, I do some charity stuff sometimes, but that's all. How did you meet Osc?"

"I live in the apartment above his. I quite literally walked into him in the lift." I glanced over at Oscar, who smiled and squeezed my hand.

Minty clapped her hands together, "that's so romantic, and he turned out to be a handsome lord who lives in a castle! It's like a fairy tale"

"I only just found out about that part," I said loudly enough for his mother to hear. I had a brief reprieve when the butler arrived with glasses of wine for both Oscar and I. I sipped mine gratefully, and listened to one of the men tell everyone about some gossip regarding a minor royal.

Oscar turned to me, "would you like the guided tour?"

"That would be great." He took my glass, and placed it on a side table, before standing, and telling the others that he was going to show me around. His mother appeared to have swallowed something sour, given how pursed her lips were.

"Your mother didn't like me," I whispered as soon as we were out of the room.

"She doesn't like anyone, even thinks the Queen's a bit common, so don't take it personally. Now can you see why I wanted to call you 'a friend'?"

"Yes. The others seem nice though."

"They are. Don't worry about mother. She won't be around much this weekend. Now, this is the gallery, that's a Turner on the wall." I stood looking at it, Oscar behind me, clasping my shoulders as I gazed at the picture of a idyllic rural scene. We moved down the gallery, stopping at each painting as he explained the artist and the subject. We stopped in front of a Raphael, and Oscar rested his chin on my shoulder, his hands clasped around my waist, as he stood behind me, telling me the story of the painting. He seemed far more affectionate and tactile than I was used to, and I found myself really enjoying his company. I decided to ask him about the addiction his mother mentioned another time.

"Have you shown her your Faberge collection yet?" A loud voice boomed out. A tall, ruggedly handsome man came striding towards us. "It's his normal chat up line, you know, come look at my pretty eggs," the man teased, smirking at Oscar, who punched him playfully on the arm.

"No I haven't yet, and anyway, I don't need to chat her up, I've done that bit already. I was just showing her my paintings."

"Beware if he offers to show you his etchings," he carried on, before offering his hand, "Darius Cavendish. Delighted to meet you." I shook his outstretched hand firmly.

"Pleased to meet you Darius. How do you two know each other?"

"Best friends since prep school. Went to Eton and Oxford together too. Can't seem to shake the miserable old bugger off, no matter where I go." Darius grinned as Oscar punched him again. "I have to say, Elle, I have never seen a girl stand up to Osc's medusa of a mother before. Most girls wither in front of her. Well done for holding it together. Don't let her bother you."

"I don't intimidate easily, thankfully." I replied. Oscar slipped his arm around my shoulders.

"This is the one that stood up to Porenski and called him out on some dodgy tactics," he said proudly. "More than a match for mother."

"Of course, so this is her," said Darius, realisation dawning, "oh well, you will definitely be able to keep the old girl in her place. Oscar told me about that a couple of weeks ago. Has Porenski forgiven you yet?"

"Oh yes, he engaged my firm last week." I said.

"He wanted Elle on his side, that's why," said Oscar.

"Quite a coup for you. Bet your bosses are pleased. Anyway, I wanted to come and warn Oscar, your mother knows about Lucinda Rothschild and Theo splitting up." Darius looked serious.

Oscar groaned. "How did she find out?"

"Lady Rothschild I gather. Just thought forewarned was forearmed. She'll be particularly unpleasant to Elle this weekend."

"Who's Lucinda Rothschild?" I asked

"My mother's idea of the perfect wife. Only problem is that she's pig ugly and hideously fat," said Oscar.

"But she has a title and a bank in the family," interjected Darius, "so the lazy eye and thunder thighs are just a little inconvenience, and apart from the fact that you would end up with ugly kids, did I mention that she has a moustache?"

I giggled, "poor girl doesn't sound like she has much going for her."

"About a trillion quid probably helps," said Darius, "the clues in the surname."

"If you were a bit short maybe, but I'm kind of assuming that Oscar's pretty comfortable." Oscar hugged me, and grinned at Darius.

"She's priceless isn't she?" Oscar said, giving me a loud, wet kiss on the cheek. "Come see my pretty eggs, then we'll see if we can fit you out with a suit of armour for pre-dinner drinks with my ever toxic mother."

"Seat Elle between you and me Osc, that way we can both look after her," said Darius, sympathy in his eyes. He headed back to the drawing room, while Oscar steered me into what he described as the 'garden room'. It was lined with glass cases along the walls, and had enormous French windows at the far end.

He pulled me towards one of the cases. "Have you ever seen a Faberge egg?" I stared at the collection of elaborately decorated eggs. Their jewel like colours enhanced by the subtle but clever lighting inside the cabinets. Each one was probably worth a fortune, and I was looking at a collection of six.

"They're exquisite. Takes my breath away how perfect they are. I thought they were really rare, yet you have six."

"Forty two exist, and these six are among the best examples. My grandfather bought them from Lenin when he was desperate for cash after the Russian revolution. By the way, Ivan doesn't know I have them, he would probably kill for them, so I prefer you not to reveal their existence."

"Of course. I won't say a word." Oscar stroked my back softly as I took in the beauty of the eggs, marvelling at the intricacy of the workmanship. After a while, I moved around the cabinets, feasting my eyes on the objects d'art they held.

"Come, we need to start getting ready for dinner," said Oscar, as he led me upstairs.

Chapter 11

Oscar's bedroom was dominated by an enormous four poster bed, covered with heavy, red drapes. The room was large, with two huge mahogany wardrobes, and a matching chest of drawers. The only modern items in the room were a phone, and a flat screen television perched on top of a chest.

"Shower or bath?" Oscar asked with a sexy smile.

"Shower please. I need to wash this dust out of my hair. It's starting to itch."

"Can I wash it for you?"

"Ok, if you want to." I was surprised at his request, but quite happy to share a shower, although I'd heard that old houses had seriously bad plumbing. He led me through a door into a modern, stylish, black marble bathroom. I could feel his breath on my neck as he unzipped my dress, sliding it off my shoulders gently. He stood behind me as he undid my bra, sliding his hands over my breasts as soon as they were freed. I stepped out of my shoes before slipping my dress, tights and knickers off in one move. I stood completely naked in front of him.

"You appear to still be dressed," I purred. I undid the buttons of his shirt while he pressed kisses along my jaw. After kicking off his shoes, he shed the rest of his clothes, and switched on the shower.

The hot water felt wonderfully soothing, pummelling my tense shoulders in a luxuriously fast flow from a large rainwater style shower head. Oscar massaged a blob of shampoo into my scalp, his firm, square fingers covering every inch, washing the grime of the day away. He tipped my head back slightly to rinse, then repeated the process, spreading the scented shampoo through the lengths of my hair, lathering it thoroughly, until it was squeaky clean.

He surprised me by conditioning it, combing the conditioner through patiently and carefully. He left it to soak in while he washed the rest of my body with a sweetly scented shower gel. He kneaded my shoulders, releasing the knots of tension with probing thumbs. I felt myself relax for the first time since six o'clock that morning.

When I was clean, I proceeded to do the same for Oscar, shampooing his hair, before lathering his entire body. As I knelt down to massage his calves and feet, I came face to face with his impressive erection. Without touching it, I caught the tip in my lips, and lightly sucked just the very end, which made his legs buckle slightly, and his hands slapped against the walls of the shower for support. I swirled my tongue over the taut skin, and he groaned loudly.

"I have to have you" he declared, pulling out of my mouth, and darting out of the shower to rifle through a drawer for a condom. He unrolled it onto himself, and stepped back into the steamy enclosure.

"Turn around, I want to take you from behind." No sooner had I turned to face the wall, and bend over, I felt him nudging into me. He reached around to massage my clitoris as he slowly thrust back and forth, circling his hips to wring maximum pleasure. With the head of his dick repeatedly hitting my g spot, I felt the familiar sensation of an impending orgasm.

He must have felt it too, as he sped up slightly, and muttered, "let go, come all over my cock, I want to feel your cunt juice dripping all over me." His carnal words, spoken in his upperclass deep voice, sent me over the edge, and I pulsed around him, crying out as my orgasm raged through my body. I felt him swell and let go, pressing deep inside me as he lost control of his body. His arms snaked around my waist, and he rested his cheek against my back as we both basked in post orgasmic bliss.

After a few moments, he planted a kiss on my back, and holding the condom in place, pulled out of me, before removing it and tying a knot.

"God you're sexy, I don't think I could ever get enough of you," he said, grabbing the shower gel to rewash us both. He stepped out of the shower while I rinsed the conditioner from my hair, and held out a large, warm towel for me. He wrapped it around me, and handed me a smaller one for my head. As I towel dried my hair, he began to shave. He used an old fashioned looking razor and shaving brush, lathering soap from a bowl.

"Enjoying the show?" He asked as I watched him drawing the blade over his face in confident strokes.

"I've never watched anyone shave before," I admitted.

"Never?"

"Nope." I watched as he finished off and wiped the remaining foam with a towel. Still wrapped up, I wandered into his bedroom to look for my weekend bag, which contained my hairdryer and brushes.

"Your things are probably in the bottom drawer of my chest, that's where Jones normally puts things when he unpacks. Your clothes will be in the left hand wardrobe." Oscar called out. I found my dryer, and carefully blow dried my hair, before putting on some makeup and perfume. I had bought my trusty little black dress to wear to dinner, and teamed it with black stockings and black heels.

"Very nice," said Oscar appreciatively, as he looked me up and down while deftly tying his tie. I did a little twirl for him.

"You sure this is ok?" I asked.

"Perfect."

Oscar held my arm as we walked into the 'sitting room', as he called it, for pre-dinner drinks. About half of the others were already there, with no sign of Oscar's mother. Oscar handed me a gin and tonic from a tray on a side table, and we joined Darius, and his wife, Arabella, as Oscar wanted to introduce me properly.

Arabella was a sweet girl, and I got the impression she had been with Darius a long time. She too teased Oscar about his overbearing mother, and her determination to pair him off with Lucinda Rothschild, who she referred to as 'shrek'.

Minty came over with her partner, who introduced himself as Thomas Darlington as he shook my hand warmly. He was ruggedly handsome, with a rugby player's physique, and a wayward mop of blonde hair. He stared pointedly at my chest as he spoke, only raising his eyes when Minty dug him in the ribs with her elbow, which Oscar seemed to think was quite funny.

"He's such a boy, you'll have to forgive him," she muttered as the men got engrossed in a conversation about rugby. "Anyone would think he'd never seen a pair of tits before. Bloody overgrown schoolboys."

I laughed, "last time I went out, an elderly, redhaired lesbian did the same thing. At least Thomas is male, so it's a step up."

Minty hooted with laughter, "that's not so bad then. At least I don't have any worries about Thomas batting for the home team. There isn't a man alive more fascinated by boobs than him."

The other three couples arrived soon after, and Minty introduced them to me, giving me some background information about each couple. Although they were all 'posh', everyone seemed really warm and friendly, with none of the snobbery exhibited by Oscar's mother. I began to relax and enjoy myself.

"What do you think of Conniscliffe?" Arabella asked.

"Beautiful so far, although I haven't had a chance to look around much yet. Hopefully I'll see more tomorrow."

"The gardens are lovely this time of year. Are you shooting tomorrow?"

"Oscar said he'd teach me. I've never tried it before."

"I don't like shooting much, so I just watch Darius," she confided, "nobody minds if you don't join in."

"I promised I'd try it, but if it's not for me, then at least I can say I've tried."

I carried on making small talk with the girls until Oscar slipped his arm around my shoulders, and pecked my cheek.

"I don't think we should wait any longer for mother, shall we head through to the dining room?" I breathed a sigh of relief that his mother wouldn't be joining us for dinner.

It was short lived as her strident voice called out, "Oscar! I need you to call that odious friend of yours this weekend." She came sweeping into the room. My heart sank.

"What odious friend and why?" Oscar said, frowning.

"Podunky, or whatever his name is. The church newsletter is going to be late because of him. It's just not good enough Oscar."

"I don't understand how Ivan has anything at all to do with the church newsletter."

"I'll tell you during dinner. We are late getting seated as it is," she declared, as she led everyone out of the room, and into the adjacent dining room.

The table looked magnificent dressed with silverware, crystal, and dainty floral centrepieces. The room itself was decorated in deep blue, with acres of gilding, and vast, heavily swagged curtains covering the four large windows that ran along one side. Oscar held me close, and steered me towards the far end of the table, seating me in the first chair next to the large carver at the head. Darius sidled up beside me, and after seating Arabella further down, took the chair next to me. Oscar's mother took the remaining end position down the table, so was about as far away from me as it was possible to get.

Jones arrived to pour water and wine, and ensure everyone was ready before the first course was served.

"You were telling me about a problem with St Augustine's newsletter mother," said Oscar.

"Yes. I had Mrs Smith on the telephone. Apparently that dreadful man is now her employer, and he sent the most horrible woman down to the company to practically hound Mrs Smith out of her job. Well, the point is, this nasty woman ripped, positively ripped, the piece Mrs Smith was typing, out of her typewriter, and forced her to abandon it. As a result, the reverend's article on spring flowers in Derwent wood isn't ready for publication."

"I see," said Oscar, refusing to catch my eye. I felt his foot nudging me under the table. "Could she not have done it after work?"

His mother gave him a 'don't be stupid' look. "Of course not, Friday nights are patchwork club, besides, she's always done it at work. They have plenty of paper and a typewriter. She's terribly upset, said the woman made her cry, and totally belittled her. Ivan needs to be told, Mrs Smith is the lifeblood of that firm, they'd fall apart without her."

"I doubt very much if Ivan would take my advice on the matter," said Oscar, trying not to smirk.

"You may be right. Mrs Smith said that the girl that turned up was like a gangster's moll, totally took over, and said Ivan had sent her to do it. Probably sleeping with him. Women like that will do anything for money. Even said she was his lawyer! As if a man like Podunky would engage a young woman as his counsel. Ridiculous that she thought anyone would even believe her."

I felt Darius shift in the chair next to me, and I desperately wanted to find out if he'd caught on. I glanced slyly at him, and saw him trying not to smile. Oscar's foot nudged me again, as he looked straight ahead at his mother.

"You could always type it up mother," said Oscar, "you can use the computer in my study, it won't take long. If its urgent...." He trailed off as his mother gave him a death stare.

"Don't be so ridiculous. That's Mrs Smith's job. Although it will delay the newsletter, and she said she won't be able to do it next week as the trollop will still be there. It's a total disaster, that's why I want you to call Ivan, and tell him how important this is."

"Would you like me to type it up for you tomorrow morning? If Oscar shows me where his computer is, it won't take me long," I offered, prompting an incredulous look from Oscar.

"That's very kind of you to offer," replied Lady Golding, "I suppose there are some advantages to having office experience. Are you sure you can do it?"

"I'm sure I can. Do you have the article here?"

She had the grace to look sheepish, "yes, the reverend photocopied it, along with the rest of the leaflet so that I could check the content."

"Elle, it's your weekend off, you don't have to do this," said Oscar.

"It's really no bother, and if it helps out...." I trailed off, seeing the amused look on Oscar's face.

We were interrupted by the arrival of the soup, carried in by uniformed servers. We all began to eat. "I've never seen a gorgon disarmed so quickly," whispered Darius, "well done. Round one to you."

Thankfully, the gorgon left me alone after that, but she just had to mention Lucinda bloody Rothschild.

"I hear Lucinda called off her engagement to Theo Goldsmith. Did you hear about that dear?" She said to Oscar. The table went quiet.

"Yes I did, mother, and don't go getting any ideas. The girl is hideous."

"I'm sure I could help her improve her figure," she said, "and a Golding-Rothschild partnership would be very fruitful."

"The answer's no. If that dreadful creature was installed here, I'd never visit again. Please refrain from discussing it again mother, besides, it's rather rude to discuss marriage when my girlfriend is sitting beside me do you not think?" I saw the anger written all over Oscar's face as he spoke. Even his mother withered slightly under his glare.

"Oh be reasonable," she said, "it's your duty to marry well."

"I'll marry well mother, but it won't be Lucinda Rothschild, I can tell you that now, so stop getting your hopes up."

His mother gave up, and began to talk to Bunty about Oscar's sister's trip to Italy. I stroked Oscars leg under the table with my foot, and gave him a supportive smile.

"Round two to Osc. The Gorgon's not having a good night," laughed Darius. "She can't even take it out on you, 'cos she wants her stupid newsletter. Outflanked methinks."

"Why do you think she's a lawyer? I've never met such a good strategist," Oscar said proudly, "she got me chasing around after her. I even got up early to catch her at our gym. I've never done anything like that before."

"Oh Oscar, you must be in love," squealed Minty, clapping her hands together, "you're exhibiting all the signs." Oscar just cleared his throat, and looked embarrassed.

The main course arrived, letting Oscar off the hook. It was minted spring lamb, which Oscar told me had come from one of the farms on the estate. It was meltingly gorgeous, served with new potatoes and steamed vegetables from the kitchen garden. A rich, full bodied red wine was served to accompany it, setting off the flavour of the lamb to perfection.

"Are you a wine buff?" I asked Oscar.

He nodded, "there are huge wine cellars under the castle, and I'm fairly well versed in the vintages we hold. Are you interested in wine?"

"Only insofar as I enjoy drinking it," I said, making him smile.

"So are you enjoying that Chateau Lafite that you're currently drinking?"

"I had no idea," I gasped, "I knew it was refined, but that's as far as my knowledge goes."

"Stick with me kid, I have nice wine," he teased, making me giggle. The rest of the meal passed without incident. I listened to the various conversations around the table, rather than talk too much, and possibly say the wrong thing. I envied the easy confidence of my companions, their place in the world assured from birth. I wished that I hadn't had to work so hard to fight my way out of my own birthplace, and carry the sense of inadequacy around on my shoulders.

Oscar was watching as I mulled it all over in my mind. "Are you ok?" He asked.

"Yes fine thanks. The lamb was gorgeous."

"We have sticky toffee pudding with a glorious Beaumes de Venise. Chef always makes that particular pudding whenever Darius comes over. It's his favourite."

Darius looked over at the mention of his name, and said "Oscar knows how to spoil me."

The dessert was indeed fabulous, and the wine, perfect. I sat back in my seat with a contented sigh, waving away the cheese course, as I was too full.

"I think we'll take coffee in the drawing room," Oscar instructed the butler, who nodded in reply.

Oscar's mother stood, "I'm retiring now, enjoy the rest of your evening." People muttered their good nights to her, and she left.

As soon as she was gone, there was a palpable sense of relief in the room. "Party time!" Declared Darius, as Oscar visibly relaxed. We all headed back to the drawing room, where cups of coffee were waiting for us. I sank into a sofa, and sipped my coffee gratefully. The wine had been fabulous, but there had been a lot of it, and I was grateful for a chance to sober up a little.

"Jones, we need champagne please," yelled Oscar. Within five minutes, Jones wheeled in a trolley containing ice buckets of champagne and crystal glasses. He opened two of the bottles expertly, and poured ten glasses.

"Will that be all for tonight sir?"

"Yes, thank you," said Oscar, as he wandered over to a cabinet, and switched on some music. As Amy Winehouse sang about going back to black, a couple of the girls got up to dance. Darius grabbed my hand and pulled me up to join in. He didn't have Oscar's easy grace, but we had fun. Oscar was dancing with Minty, and if I hadn't been busy concentrating on staying upright in my heels, I would have loved to be able to sit and just watch him in feminine carnal appreciation. He had shed his jacket and tie, and his shirt sleeves were rolled up. In my slightly inebriated state of mind, he looked extremely yummy.

Chapter 12

We danced until around midnight, changing partners with every song. We also polished off another four bottles of champagne. As people began to sit down, I decided to join them. I had only sipped my champagne, but still felt a touch light headed. Oscar sat down next to me and slipped his arm around my shoulder before pressing a wet kiss to my cheek.

"You tired baby?" He inquired.

"No, I'm having a good time. My feet are a bit sore though, I've been wearing heels since six this morning."

"Do you think you could keep them on a little longer? They're very, erm, nice," he said, gazing at my shoes with longing.

"Just for you," I said, batting my lashes at him, "as long as I stay sitting down."

The others joined us on the sofas, and Oscar turned the music down.

"I've never seen Oscar like this," declared Minty, who seemed to have no brain to mouth filter, "he's totally in love. I can tell." Oscar just hugged me a bit tighter, and planted another kiss on my nose. He was clearly tipsy, and was behaving like an enthusiastic Labrador, rather than the uptight and buttoned up businessman I was used to. I decided I liked drunk and soppy Oscar.

"Forgot to tell you, my study is two doors along from the garden room, next to the kitchen. You always wake up before me, so best I tell you now." Oscar rambled on, trying to describe where to find paper and the printer in his home office.

"Party game time," called out Hartey, who I'd found out earlier, had got his nickname from his surname of Spencer-Harte. "I suggest charades if you're not all too pissed."

"Way too pissed," groaned Darius, "how about truth or dare?"

Minty clapped her hands and squealed, "I love that game."

112

Oscar got up and rummaged around in a drawer before returning with a dice."First six is the first up, second six is the questioner," he said, handing the dice to me. I rolled it, and it landed on two. The next person rolled, and it went around until it reached Oscar, who threw the first six. The dice carried on until it reached my turn. I threw the second six.

"So Oscar, truth or dare?" I asked, smirking at him.

"Truth."

"Ok, what's your full title and name?"

He took a deep breath, "Lord Oscar Algernon Harold Maximilien Golding, Lord of the manor of Derwent, and Knight of the Garter." He blushed as I sniggered.

"Harold? What on earth made them call you that?"

"I gather it's a family name. They all are, and it's a big, Jewish family."

The dice continued, Darius threw the next six."Truth or dare Elle?" I weighed up my options. I didn't know the types of dares they did, but I also didn't want any probing questions. I decided to go with questions, fairly confident of my ability to deflect anything I didn't want to answer.

"Truth please."

Darius stared at me for a moment, a devious look in his eye, "are you wearing stockings or tights?"

That was easy, "stockings." The men all groaned. The dice continued. Minty got the next six, and Darius chose to perform a dare.

"I dare you to kiss Oscar on the lips," she grinned. Darius pulled a face.

"I'm not paying a forfeit, so brace yourself Golding," he said as he grabbed Oscar's face, and planted a big wet kiss on his lips. Both men made a big show of pulling faces and scrubbing their lips.

"You're a shit kisser Cavendish."

"You have bad breath Golding, otherwise I'd have snogged you properly."

"What's the forfeit?" I asked.

"If you choose to forfeit, the punishment is decided by the host, in tonight's case, Osc," replied Darius, raising his eyebrows in mock horror, "and he's a sadistic bugger."

The game carried on for a few more rounds until it was again Oscar's turn, with Minty as the questioner.

"Dare," chose Oscar.

"I dare you to tell Elle that you love her," said Minty.

Oscar turned to me, and quickly said, "I love you," before turning back to Minty, "ok? Next person." *Hmm, he didn't mean it then.*

It carried on. Eventually it was my turn to perform a truth or dare. "Dare please." I said to Thomas who was my questioner this time.

"I dare you to get your tits out," he leered with a lewd look on his face. All the men looked at me expectantly, apart from Oscar who was frowning.

I laughed, "I'm sorry boys, but my girls are for Oscar's eyes only, so I'm going to throw myself at his mercy and declare a forfeit." Thomas looked disappointed, while Oscar had a carnal expression.

"And with that ladies and gentlemen, I'm gonna bid you all goodnight, and make this naughty girl pay her forfeit. In. Full." I squealed as he grabbed me and threw me over his shoulder before carrying me to his room, caveman style.

When we got to his bedroom, he set me down gently, and went over to lock the door. I stood still, watching him as he moved around the room turning on the bedside lamps, before switching off the main light. He kicked off his shoes and socks before removing his trousers and undoing his shirt. I didn't move as he perched on the side of the bed and raked his eyes over me.

"I want you to slowly lift up your dress, and pull down your knickers just enough to flash me. I just want a glimpse, nothing more."

I edged the hem of my dress up slowly, running my fingers over my thighs as I went. Aroused by his suggestion, and what it would lead to, I squeezed my thighs together as my dress inched upwards. His breathing hitched as I uncovered the tops of my stockings.

When my dress was lifted to my waist, I took the front of my black lace knickers, and edged them down, showing myself to him. I was already hot and slick, turned on by his sexy appreciation. After a moment, I pulled my knickers back up, and smoothed the front of my dress back down. My clit was throbbing and twitching in anticipation of what he was going to do next.

He silently beckoned me over, and bent me over his lap. I could feel his steely erection pressing against my tummy. "Your forfeit, is to spend all night as my personal sex slave. I shall tie you to the bed, and I will fuck you whenever and however I want for the next eight hours. Is that clear?"

"Yes Oscar."

"You will address me as Sir tonight. Is that clear?"

"Yes sir."

He slowly pulled my dress up, to expose my lace clad behind. He pulled my knickers down exquisitely slowly before running his warm hands repeatedly over my buttocks. His fingers dipped down to my clit, and he teased me for a while before returning to my backside. "You're soaked. Tell me Elle, are you wet for me, or did the thought of all those men seeing your naked breasts turn you on?"

"Only you sir," I replied, wondering if he was into spanking. It certainly wasn't my thing.

"Good girl. Now, I want you to go to the bathroom and afterwards, take your knickers off. Only your knickers. Understand?"

"Yes sir." He stood me upright, and I went to the bathroom quickly, leaving my knickers in there. When I returned, Oscar was leaning back against the pillows, naked, lazily stroking his cock.

"Stand there, and pull your dress up." I did has he asked, exposing myself to him. "Now pull your pussy lips apart, and show me your clit." As I did his bidding, my clitoris twitched, and throbbed with arousal. He stared intently, "do you like to be looked at?"

"Only by you," I replied, hyper aware of my throbbing clit, and rock hard nipples. I was desperate to be fucked, but also desperate to continue this sensual torment.

"Take off your dress, and bra. Leave just your stockings and shoes on." Oscar ordered. I pulled the dress over my head, and unclasped my bra, sliding it slowly down my arms. My nipples stood to attention, as hard as bullets.

"Turn around, and stand with your feet apart." I did as he asked. "Good girl, now bend over and touch the floor. I want to see your wet cunt from behind."

I could see him through my legs, stroking himself as his eyes bored into me. I began to ache to have him inside me, pounding me to orgasm. "I think you want me to fuck you. Your cunt is practically dripping. I think being watched turns you on." His voice was low, very sexy, and extremely authoritative.

"Please Oscar." *I'm not above begging.* I could see him speed his strokes, one hand caressing his body as the other rubbed the head of his cock, before moving to pump the shaft. I watched as he approached his climax. His hand pumping faster and faster, until he groaned as semen oozed from the tip of his engorged cock. It was the most erotic sight I'd ever seen.

I felt strangely bereft, and very desperate for some relief, as my clit was actually starting to hurt from it's extreme arousal. "Stand upright, and come over here," he breathed, in his seductive baritone. I sashayed over, standing beside him with my legs slightly parted, and my clit throbbing wildly. He jumped off the bed, and pulled back the covers, before standing behind me. I could feel his breath on my shoulder, as his lips hovered before planting an oh-so-soft kiss, which ignited my entire skin. His fingers traced down my spine, down the crease of my buttocks, and dipped into my soaking sex.

"Lay on the bed, on your back," he whispered. I did as he asked, and watched at he opened his bedside cupboard and pulled out a pair of handcuffs and some condoms. I expected him to cuff my wrists, but he surprised me by clipping one cuff around my left ankle, and the other to the bedpost.

"No escaping for the next seven hours," he said, smiling sexily. I smiled back, relieved to see the condoms. He climbed onto the bed, and straddled my hips, sitting back to look down at me. His cock was resting on my tummy, still thick and heavy, even in it's semi flaccid state.

He traced featherlight circles around each of my nipples in turn, before leaning forward to kiss me deeply, his tongue exploring my mouth, before pressing tiny kisses down my neck to suckle my nipple hard. I arched off the bed, and pressed my thighs together, trying to calm my aroused clitoris. Oscar moved off me and pulled my legs apart. With his fingers, he held my labia apart, causing my clit to be exposed.

"Oh baby, I could tease you for hours," he taunted as he slid a finger inside me, carefully avoiding my exposed clitoris he slowly pumped his finger in and out, curling it slightly to massage my g spot. Before I had a chance to come, his finger stopped, and he moved back to straddle me again.

"Keep your legs open," he ordered, "I want your mouth round my cock first. He slid forward to ease his hardening cock into my open mouth, teasing me with just the tip. I swirled my tongue over it, licking and sucking it, willing him to give me more.

He began by just thrusting the very end of his cock into my welcoming mouth, the thrusts getting deeper and deeper, until it was a struggle to get my lips around the thick shaft, and I could taste his pre-come. He pulled away, making me whimper, and turned his attention back to my pussy, teasing it, lightly tapping my desperate clit, until I was practically convulsing with need.

"Please Oscar, I really need you to fuck me, please," I begged shamelessly, writhing and tugging on the handcuff round my ankle. I even tried to slip my hand down to bring myself off, but he caught my wrists and pinned them above my head, kissing me deeply, as I writhed with need.

He held my wrists as he continued his sensual torment, tracing his tongue down to my breast, and nibbling at my nipple gently with his teeth.

"I'm going to fuck you now, but you're not allowed to come. Understand?" *Fat chance of that!*

"I'll try," I panted. He rolled on a condom, and positioned himself between my legs.

He nudged into me slowly, and in my sensitised state, I felt every ridge of his cock as he stretched me inside, filling me, easing the aching his teasing caused. He stopped.

"Don't come," he reminded me. If he'd have taken a deep breath at that moment, I would have lost control. He stayed still for a few more moments, then began to pound me at a primal, aggressively fast pace, pinning my hips to the bed with his hands.

I came with a scream, my orgasm so intense that I saw stars. He ignored me as I lay pulsing and convulsing around him as he continued to fuck me into next week.

As my orgasm began to subside, he swivelled his hips and changed angles to allow his cock to rub repeatedly over my g spot. Another orgasm began brewing, and I barely had time to take a breath before it overwhelmed me, and I came again, arching my back off the bed.

"Dirty little slut, coming all over my cock. Your filthy cunt is dripping all over me. That hungry little cunt is milking my big cock, it's so greedy for big cock. You want all the boys to come and look at your cunt? Queue up to service it? All of them to fuck you hard, rub their cocks inside you till all you can do is drip cunt juice over them and come over and over. Is that what you like? Them all wanting to look at your dirty little clit?"

Then I came again, so hard it hurt. My insides clenching with such force that I cried out. Oscar came with a shout, pressing into me, as we both shuddered and tensed. He rested his forehead on mine as we both recovered from our explosive orgasms, then gave me a chaste kiss before gently pulling out of me, and flopping down on the bed beside me.

"I do believe you came, naughty girl," he said as he nuzzled my neck.

"It wasn't my fault," I said, "it was that big cock of yours did it." He seemed pleased, and I felt him smile against my neck.

"Well, this big cock needs a few minutes to recover, then we're going to see if he can make you scream again. We have all night, remember."

"I've never come three times before, I'm not sure if I can again." I said, wondering if he was going to unclip my ankle. I felt sleepy, sated, and a bit drunk.

"We'll just have to find out. I have a vibrator to help," he replied.

"Can I ask you something?"

"Of course."

"Why haven't you ever gone down on me?"

Oscar shifted back to look at me. "I just don't like it. Does that bother you?"

"It's a little strange."

"Don't take it personally. I've never liked it. Just a quirk of mine."

"Like the shoe fetish?" I kissed the tip of his nose.

"The shoe fetish is a big quirk of mine," he smiled, "can I take you shoe shopping? I'd love to buy you some Laboutins or Jimmy Choos, then fuck you when you're wearing them."

"Hmm, I think I'd like that," I said, more excited at the prospect of the shopping than the sex. I stretched lazily, and turned to face Oscar, running my hand over his lean ribs. " I'm still horny for you, ready for round two yet?"

"I thought you were meant to be the sex slave, you demanding little girl," murmured Oscar, tweaking my nipple before reaching over for another condom.

Round two proved to be rather passionate lovemaking. With my ankle still shackled to the bed, we stuck to missionary, Oscar holding me tight, and wringing every last drop of pleasure from me. He even managed to squeeze the elusive fourth orgasm out of me, pressing the vibrator to my clit as his cock massaged me inside.

Finally sated, he wrapped his arms around me, pulled the covers over us, and fell asleep. I lay there awhile in the dark, contemplating how far I'd come from the humble council flat. I'd spent many years worrying about not fitting in, or my accent and background holding me back, and yet here I was, laying next to my beautiful lover, in a castle on a hill. I held that thought as I drifted off with a smile on my face.

Chapter 13

Damn the curse of the earlybird, I thought, when I awoke at six. I looked around for the key to the cuff round my ankle, and found it on the bedside table. Oscar was out for the count, his sculptured lips slightly parted, and his beautiful face relaxed and serene. I undid the handcuff, and rubbed my ankle before sliding out of bed, and padding over to the bathroom. I clipped my hair up, and took a quick, perfunctory shower, before dressing in jeans and a fitted t shirt. I slipped out of the room, and went in search of the kitchen.

The castle was enormous, and it was difficult to get my bearings with the numerous corridors. I found my way back to the garden room, and carried on down that hallway, trying to remember Oscar's drunken directions from the night before. I tried the next door along from the garden room, which turned out to be a store cupboard. Carrying on, I found his study. It looked very similar to his office at work. A vast, mahogany desk dominated the room, flanked by three large bookcases which held a mixture of biographies and books on business and investment theory.

I switched on the computer, and picked up the article that Lady Golding had left for me. The handwriting was pretty awful, but decipherable, and the rest of the newsletter had already been badly typed by Marion. I placed it back on the desk, and went in search of the kitchen.

I pushed open a door, and found a large, rather old fashioned kitchen, with wooden cupboards, and a huge, wooden table in the centre. A middle aged woman, with her grey hair piled into a bun, stood at the sink.

"Good morning, I'm Elle, I hope you don't mind if I make myself a cup of tea," I said.

"Mrs Dunton, pleased to meet you. I'll make it for you, which tea do you prefer?" She dried her hands and filled the kettle, before placing it on a vast aga to boil. I asked for English breakfast.

"Are you the cook here?"

"Yes dear, I do breakfasts and lunches. There are three of us altogether, but I'm an early riser, so prefer to do the morning shift," she said pleasantly, "you're up early."

"Always am. I'm an early bird too. I promised Lady Golding I'd help with her newsletter, so I thought I'd get on with that. It was a late night last night, so I expect the others will be having a lay in."

"Shall I bring your tea along to the study?"

"That would be lovely, if you don't mind that is."

"Not at all. You go and get settled, and I'll bring it as soon as the kettles boiled."

I went back to the study, and pulled up the word program. Marion had been typing on normal A4, in portrait, so I started with that. Within five minutes, Mrs Dunton arrived with a tray holding a teapot, cup and saucer, and the other accompaniments. She placed it on the desk and watched me type.

"Don't you type fast? Are you trained in secretarial?"

"No, but I do it all day, every day, so I'm as fast as a good secretary. Have you worked here long?" I stopped typing, and poured my tea.

"Goodness, almost 45 years. Don't know where the time goes. Started as a maid when I was sixteen, and the cook back then trained me up to work in the kitchen."

"It's a beautiful place to work. I'm hoping Oscar will show me around the gardens today."

"The gardens are very special. Make sure he shows you the white garden, it's at it's best right now." She smiled kindly, and left before I could pump her for information about Oscar.

I went back to the newsletter and finished the article, spellchecked it, and read through it. Some of the Latin names looked a bit wrong, so I pulled up the RHS website, and checked them, altering the spelling of two. I looked over Marion's sheets, which were littered with spelling mistakes and typos, and decided to re-type them so that the newsletter would all be in the same font.

Another half hour later, I was prettying it all up with some nice heading fonts, and experimenting with different leaflet formats, before printing off three different options for Lady Golding.

I was just clipping the papers together when she swept into the room, "Mrs Dunton said you were in here. Did you manage to work Oscar's computer?" I handed her the finished newsletters.

"I didn't know how you wanted it to look, so I gave you three different options," I said, smiling as she perused the papers.

"Oh these are superb," she declared, shocking me to the bone, "no spelling mistakes either, for a change, oh, hang on, the reverend spelt 'jonquil' differently."

"I checked that on the RHS website, and corrected it," I admitted, "I didn't know it meant daffodil, but my Latin is good enough to spot dodgy spelling."

"Excellent. I'll have the driver take these into town tomorrow for printing. They'll be ready in a fortnight."

"I can email your chosen design to them to save a journey," I offered. She looked incredulous.

"Let me get more tea, and I'll sit and choose one." Lady Golding walked off in search of Mrs Dunton, and I marvelled at how different she was in daylight.

She returned after a few minutes, and sat at the desk, opposite me, looking through the three formats. "Which one do you think?"

"The A4 portrait style," I said, reaching over to show her which one I meant, "what's the name of your printer?" I opened the web browser, and noting that she couldn't see the screen, clicked on the history. The usual BBC news, Facebook, and a few bouncy boobs porn sites were listed, but nothing of real interest, apart from a visit to narcotics anonymous two weeks ago. I quickly closed the history and typed the name of the printer into the search engine.

It took five minutes to order the newsletter, and attach the file, send it and pay using my PayPal account. Lady Golding was clearly delighted to have the problem solved by 8.30 am.

"I'm sorry if I made you uncomfortable last night," she said suddenly. I sipped my tea, and regarded her intently.

"I understand your being suspicious of Oscar's girlfriends. There's a lot of wealth in your family, a lot to protect. I get that. In my defence, I didn't know about it when Oscar pursued me. I thought he worked in a bank."

"You're very different from the girls he's brought home before. I get the impression that you aren't angling for marriage and babies. All the previous girlfriends have been desperate for the ring on their finger."

"It's not my agenda at all Lady Golding. I know you won't understand the career girl thing, but that's who I am. It's very early days with Oscar, and I don't know him terribly well yet. I find all the accoutrements a touch intimidating to be honest."

"He was such a difficult boy growing up. Always surly and angry, yet needy and weak willed. His father and I tried to help," she sighed, "but he fought with us about almost everything. Seeing him with you last night, so calm and happy, and so eager to take care of you, well, it's nothing short of a transformation."

"You didn't seem very happy about it last night," I said, remembering her death glares.

"Envious, seeing him protecting you, looking at you the way he does," *what?* "he's still my little boy remember. Is he still asleep?"

"Sleeping like a baby, we all had a lot of champagne last night, and it knocked him out. I hope he doesn't sleep too late, I wanted him to show me around the gardens, Mrs Dunton recommended I see the white garden."

"Oh yes you must, it's putting on quite the show this year. The dry spring we've had has helped. It's really romping along with the spring flowers. Do you have a garden?"

"Sadly not. I live in the apartment above Oscar in London, even the balcony is tiny."

"We'll you can enjoy our gardens when you're here. Now, I suggest that if Oscar isn't awake by nine, you give him a shake. Mrs Dunton likes to have breakfast done and dusted by half nine." She got up, and swept out of the room. I sat back and replayed the conversation in my head, it had been like talking to a different person.

I closed down the computer, and took the tray of tea things back to the kitchen, leaving it on the huge table. Back in the bedroom, Oscar was snoring softly. I stroked his shoulder to wake him up, and he opened sleepy blue eyes. "What time is it?"

"About nine. You were out cold." He rolled onto his back, pulling me onto the bed with him.

"How did you get out of the cuff Houdini?"

"You left the key on the table. Which was lucky as you were sparko," I giggled, as he kissed my neck, his bristles tickling me.

"A dastardly escape. Oh god, I want you again. What are you doing to me Elle?"

"Turning you into a sex fiend I think. Your breakfast is almost ready downstairs. I was sent up to get you, not jump you."

"Ok, ok, I'll get up. You go down to the breakfast room, and I'll be down in ten." He jumped out of bed, and wandered naked to the bathroom. I sat on the bed, watching his slim, lithe buttocks as he moved. "I can see you staring," he said.

"I'm forming the Oscar's arse appreciation society," I replied, before getting off the bed, and going back downstairs in search of the breakfast room.

Only Darius and Arabella were up and dressed, and helping themselves to coffee when I walked in. Mrs Dunton had laid out heated tureens of bacon, sausage and scrambled egg. She came in carrying a rack of toast, which she placed on the sideboard, before checking the eggs hadn't gone rubbery. "Everyone's so late this morning," she grumbled, as she fussed around with the coffee pot. As soon as she left, I poured myself a coffee, and seeing that the others had started eating, served myself a plate of toast and eggs, and joined them at the table.

"So you're still in one piece then?" Darius said, prompting a glare from his wife.

"Oh yes, I'm fine thanks. What time did you all stay up till?"

"About half one. Paying for it now though. Is Osc up?"

"Yes I'm up," said Oscar as he walked in, and straight to the coffee pot. He shovelled some food onto a plate and sat down opposite me.

"You're looking perky this morning," said Darius slyly.

"Looking forward to the shoot this afternoon," replied Oscar, "I'm always perky before a shoot." Darius smirked. "What would you like to do this morning Elle?" Oscar asked.

"I'd like to see the white garden. Mrs Dunton highly recommended it, if that's ok."

"Thought you had to do that stupid newsletter?" Darius asked.

"Done, approved by Lady Golding, sent to the printers, and paid for," I replied.

"You saw my mother this morning?" Oscar said, frowning.

"Yes, she came and found me in your study just as I finished the newsletter. She was very nice. Different to how she was last night. We had a nice chat, and she was pleased with how I did the layout for her." The two men looked at each other.

"Are you sure it was my mother and not an imposter?" Oscar said, prompting a snort from Darius. "It's just that 'nice' and my mother are rarely in the same sentence." Darius sniggered.

"Well she was nice. She cares about you." With that, Oscar changed the subject, and began to discuss shotguns with Darius. We finished breakfast, and Oscar suggested we go for a walk.

We strolled hand in hand through the knot garden, an impossibly romantic place, flanked on three sides by ancient yew hedges. The sun shone brightly, adding to the perfection. We walked in silence, me enjoying the tranquility and peace of the place, but Oscar looked thoughtful, as if he was wrestling with something.

"Are you having a nice time?" Oscar asked suddenly, breaking the silence.

"Oh yes, everyone seems really nice and welcoming, and a lot more fun than I expected."

"I know you were nervous. I was too." He looked into the distance, rather than directly at me.

"Why would you be nervous?" I was curious.

"Because I know that you can walk away from me. You seem so strong and self contained. It makes me nervous that I could say the wrong thing again and you'd be off. I nearly laid an egg last night when mother mentioned rehab."

"What were you addicted to?"

"Cocaine. I was a heavy duty coke head. Been clean for four years now. It's why nobody does drugs around me. It started off as a party thing, only I couldn't control it. Darius could always take it or leave it. I ended up an addict."

"How did it get that bad?"

"I went from using it at the weekend, to during the week. Eventually I couldn't get out of bed without a line first. It all got hushed up by my father of course. He carted me off to some godawful place on the Isle of White to get clean. I doubt if I'd still be here if he hadn't."

"Have you ever relapsed?"

"No. I have no desire to ever go back to being an addict." He looked down at the ground, "are you shocked?"

"A bit. I thought you were into fitness and health. I'm glad you told me though. I want to get to know you." We came to a large rose arch, Oscar checked for webs, before guiding me through into the most beautiful garden I'd ever seen. White flowers of every conceivable shape and size billowed against a backdrop of deep green hedges. Oscar led me to an arbour dripping with white wisteria, and we sat down, and I breathed in the heady perfumes around me. "This is paradise," I declared.

"It is now that you're here," he said, "I want to know you better too. It always feels as though you're hiding something from me, and it makes me nervous."

I contemplated whether or not to share my insecurities with him. It was nowhere near as bad as the revelation that he'd been a junkie. I took a deep breath. "I come from a poor background." I waited for his response with baited breath.

"I knew you weren't rich, but I wouldn't have pegged you as poor. Why is it such a secret?"

"I work in one of the best law firms. All my workmates come from privileged backgrounds, public school, you know. I didn't, so I had to work ten times harder, and cover up a lot. If I didn't, I'd never have been taken on, let alone won promotions. I carry a lot of insecurities and hang ups around with me. I don't really belong in this world I live in. I sneaked in."

"Is that how you felt during dinner last night?"

"Yes, you guessed."

"Only because you looked so lost." He looked at me with such sympathy that it took every ounce of self control I possessed not to cry. "Elle, you are the most amazing woman I've ever met. You're stunningly beautiful, astoundingly clever, and the sweetest person I know. You have nothing to feel insecure or inferior about. I imagine a lot of women feel intimidated by you instead."

"I doubt that very much," I snorted.

"My receptionist does. Sulks all afternoon when you've been in," he grinned.

"I did tell you she has a crush on you."

"She's normally fine. It's only when you visit that she gets all snippy. Are your own colleagues not jealous of you?"

"Not that I've noticed," I frowned, "one secretary really doesn't like me, but all the other lawyers are men, and they just tease me about you and Ivan." Oscar looked quizzical, "they are nosy about you, and think its funny that I used to hide in the loo whenever Ivan was in," I explained. Oscar laughed.

"You used to hide from Ivan? Does he know?" I shrugged.

"I was scared of him. I'm not anymore though. I was scared of you when I first met you. You seemed so angry."

"That morning you walked into me in the lift, mother had called me, giving me a hard time, berating me for missing my narcotics anonymous meeting. I was annoyed, then as soon as I actually saw you, I was angry with myself for being such an arse. Then when I chased you into the coffee shop, she bloody phoned me again. She couldn't have worse timing if she tried."

I smiled, "spectacularly bad."

Oscar stood, and grasped my hand, "I doubt that you have a thirst for blood sports, so shall I teach you how to shoot lumps of clay? Then you can be a proper hooray Henrietta." He winked at me and smiled.

Chapter 14

Clay pigeon shooting was a lot of fun. I wasn't particularly good at it, but Oscar and Hartey patiently tutored me in how to hold and fire the gun, and how to anticipate the clay. I even managed to hit a couple. Hartey was the best shot, explaining that he grew up in the highlands where his family have an estate, and was shooting grouse and pheasants almost as soon as he was big enough to hold a shotgun. Oscar was pretty good, and only missed a few clays. I watched him as he relaxed and had fun, observing how competitive he was with Darius, and how his brows knitted together as he concentrated. I may have even drooled slightly watching his broad shoulders tense and flex as he fired his gun, and his arse in Levi's was a work of art that Michelangelo himself would be proud of.

We headed back to the house around four ish, and had coffee and cake in the sitting room. After our conversation that morning, Oscar was protective and attentive, staying close and shooting little glances over to make sure I was ok, making me all warm and fuzzy.

We headed up to Oscar's room to bathe and dress for dinner. He ran the bath while I lay down on the bed, yawning my head off.

"Is the fresh air getting to you?" Oscar asked as he wandered in.

"I'm not used to clean air. It's knocked me out a bit." I yawned again.

"We'll make it an early night tonight. Everyone looks a bit ropey after last night." I followed him into the bathroom, and stripped off my clothes. The bath looked deep and inviting, and my shoulders were sore and stiff from the recoil of the gun. I stepped in, and sank into the foam. Oscar climbed in behind me, and pulled me against his chest, resting his hands on my tummy. We lay like that for a while in companionable silence before Oscar asked, "did you enjoy the shoot?"

"Oh yes, it was fun. I wasn't too bad at it for my first go was I?"

"No. I thought you took to it really well. Most girls can't even hold the gun up, let alone control the recoil. Must be all that weight training you do. Hartey was surprised too. I bet your shoulder aches though." He soaped up his hands and began to rub my shoulders. "Can I ask you something Elle?"

"Go on."

"You said you came from a poor background. What exactly did you mean?"

I hesitated for a moment before replying. "A council flat in south London, and a single parent family, on benefits. It was grim. All I wanted was to escape and never go back." His hands stopped rubbing.

"I had no idea. You don't look like you came from something like that."

"I'll take that as a compliment. I don't look chavvy," I teased. He rinsed my shoulders and planted a soft kiss. "Can I ask you something?" I said.

"Go ahead."

"How come you're still single? Have you never fallen in love?"

"That's two questions."

"So sue me."

"In answer to question two, yes I fell in love at university, but she couldn't cope with the coke habit, and left me. I loved the drugs more than I loved her I guess. In answer to question one, I didn't meet anyone after her that I wanted to spend my life with, and I enjoyed thwarting mother's attempts at matchmaking. It became a mission of mine."

"I see."

"Have you ever been in love?"

"Not really. I went out with a boy at uni, but it didn't last. He wanted different things from life than I did, so I ended it."

"What different things did he want that drove you away?"

"He wanted to be a writer, and he thought poverty was romantic, probably because he'd never experienced it.I know full well that there's nothing remotely romantic about not being able to answer the door and hiding behind the sofa when the debt collectors call round. I didn't want that life for myself, so I bailed."

"Don't blame you. It sounds horrific."

"It was. I lived in fear of having my things taken away. It's why I never have lots of 'stuff', if I don't have it, I can't lose it. I don't get attached to material things, and I live in fear of debt. I refuse to ever borrow money. I saw what it led to."

"I'd love to take you shopping and give you lovely things. You deserve the best."

"I'm not a charity case Oscar, I earn a good living and can buy nice things for myself. Don't worry, I wouldn't embarrass you by wearing Primark clothes," I snapped, suddenly regretting sharing so much information.

"You'd look lovely whatever you wore, but you'd look fabulous in couture." He kissed my shoulder. "I don't think you're a charity case at all, certainly not when you're parked in your fancy office, with a PA doing your bidding. I love the little suits you wear to work, especially when you don't wear knickers underneath them." He reached up and tweaked my nipple.

"Sex maniac," I laughed, squirming.

As soon as we were out of the bath, we made love again on the bed, a decidedly non kinky quickie, but satisfying nonetheless. We just couldn't seem to get enough of each other's bodies, and we only stopped because it was time to dress and join Oscar's guests downstairs.

I wore my wrap dress, and a pair of heels, which I knew Oscar liked, and we made our way down to pre dinner drinks in the sitting room. The others were already there, sipping gin and tonics, and discussing the shoot. This time I felt more relaxed and confident than I had the previous evening, and I began to enjoy myself.

Lady Golding appeared, and made a beeline for me, "Elle, you look lovely dear, did you visit the garden?"

"I did, and it's stunning, like paradise on earth. All the grounds are, but the white garden took my breath away," I gushed. She looked pleased. Oscar was by my side within moments of his mother's arrival.

"Did Elle tell you she did a magnificent job with the parish newsletter. Sent it to be printed and everything," she said to Oscar.

"She mentioned that she'd done it. Won't Mrs Smith's nose be out of joint?"

"Well she complains at having to type it all, so I'm sure she'll be relieved. Did you shoot today Elle?"

"I did indeed Lady Golding. It was a lot of fun." I didn't need to admit to her that it was my first time.

"I hope your shoulder's not too sore. I find that shotguns are too heavy for me."

"She's surprisingly solid. Looks a flimsy little thing, but that kickback didn't knock her over," said Hartey, joining in the conversation, "good shot too."

Lady Golding smiled and moved off to chat to Minty and Thomas. Oscar bent down to whisper in my ear, "she likes you. I'm concerned that you're going to get lumbered with that stupid newsletter for evermore, but at least she's not clawing your eyes out." He put his arm around my shoulder, and gave me a little squeeze, before announcing that we should head into the dining room.

Dinner was a sedate affair that evening. The food and wine were as delicious as before, but everyone seemed tired. Lady Golding complemented my dress, and asked who it was designed by. Thankfully I was able to tell her it was by Diana Von Furstenburg, which was better than having to admit to wearing something from Zara. She didn't have to know it was in the sale. All the girls chatted about shopping, while the men just listened politely.

"I promised Elle a nice shopping trip soon," Oscar said to Minty.

"You make sure you hammer his bank balance," she advised me, "he's got oodles of money, best he spends a bit of it on you." I smiled. She really had no brain to mouth filter.

"I plan on spoiling her," said Oscar, looking affronted, "I'm taking her to Harrods for a splurge."

"You really don't need to," I said, "I'm perfectly capable of buying my own clothes."

"Oh you should let him," said Minty, "it's a man's way of telling you he loves you. Isn't that right Osc?"

Oscar stared into his wine glass, before saying, "yes, I suppose it is." Minty clapped her hands together, delighted, and I noticed that Darius was the only one at the table not smiling at Oscar's rather clumsy confession. The look he shot Oscar was a mixture of exasperation, and anger, and it surprised me. Even Oscar's mother seemed quite misty eyed, which also surprised me. Oscar just looked a bit pink, and embarrassed.

The subject changed to the castle, with Lady Golding regaling us all with the rather colourful history of the previous inhabitants, and the awful ways they behaved. She was a talented raconteur, and I was transfixed, listening to her. As a result, the remainder of dinner passed without incident.

After coffee in the sitting room, and with several people yawning, Oscar and I decided on an early night. It was still eleven o'clock, which for me, was fairly late, so we said goodnight, and headed upstairs.

"Did you want to stay downstairs and party?" Oscar asked, as I took my makeup off in the bathroom. He began to brush his teeth. It was all very cosy and domestic.

"I'm exhausted from all the fresh air. Felt as though I was gonna drop off at the table. Your mum was interesting though. I liked hearing about the castle."

"She's very knowledgeable," he agreed, after rinsing his mouth, "although her family were from Kent. She came to Conniscliffe when she married my father. He was the real expert on the family history." Oscar tossed his clothes into the laundry basket, and wandered into the bedroom naked.

I followed, and we got into the enormous bed, snuggling together in the centre. "I'm not too tired," I purred seductively, my hands roaming over the muscles of his chest.

"Oh good, I was worried," he said, nuzzling my neck, "I don't want you all worn out, just because of my insatiable demands."

"I thought that was the whole point of the early night?" I said, squirming as he cupped my breast. Just the slightest touch from

Oscar seemed to ignite my body, and I grew slick and hot as he kissed me. He lay on his side, one hand gently stroking my cheek, as he kissed me with lush, deep kisses, his tongue sweeping over mine in soft licks. His other hand slowly travelled down my body, exploring my skin, until it slipped between my legs to feel my arousal. With a featherlight touch, he teased my clitoris, rubbing tiny circles, until I pulled him over me. Quickly sliding on a condom, he pushed into me achingly slowly, and began moving at a leisurely pace, savouring the moment, as he held me tight, still kissing me.

He pulled himself upright, and continued his slow pace, reaching down to rub my clit. I felt the orgasm brewing inside, and unable to control it, I came with a cry. Within moments, I felt Oscar swell and let go. He stilled, and pressed into me as he came, before laying back on top of me, holding me tightly and kissing me hard.

He pulled out, and lay beside me, running his warm hands over my ribs. "What I feel for you scares me," he whispered. I stared at his beautiful face, with it's worried look, and smiled.

"Oh?" I replied. In truth, it was too early to declare undying love, but I did feel a lot for him. I liked him more and more as time went by. I felt comfortable with him, and I fancied the pants off of him. It was enough for me, and I certainly wasn't going to rock the boat by saying I didn't have the same feelings as him.

"I think I'm in love," he blurted out, scanning my face. I kissed him softly.

"Me too," I replied. He pulled me into an embrace, and held me tightly. I could feel his heart hammering in his chest, either from the exertion of our lovemaking, or the anxiety of his declaration. I could feel him smile against my neck as he nuzzled me.

"Sleep baby, you look shattered," he said, pulling away slightly. I turned onto my side, snuggled into him, and drifted off.

I don't really know what woke me, whether it was the cold, empty space beside me, or the parched mouth from the salt I put on my salmon at dinner. I lay there for a few minutes, trying to go back to sleep. It was nearly one in the morning.

I figured that my raging thirst would only get worse as the night wore on, so I swung my legs out of bed, and pulled on my robe. I padded through the dim corridors, and down the stairs to the kitchen, trying not to make any noise or wake anyone else. I walked past the garden room on my way to the end of the corridor, and heard voices coming from Oscar's study.

I heard Oscar's voice clearly. He sounded like he was begging. I could hear another voice murmuring something, but it was too quiet to hear properly. I stood at the door, trying to listen, when I heard Oscar clearly announce that he was coming. My blood ran cold, and I stood, immobile, unsure what to do. I heard grunts, and sex type noises coming from behind the door, and a man's voice saying something about daring to fuck a commoner, which spurred me into action. If Oscar was screwing someone else, I needed to know now, rather than further down the road, when I had deeper feelings for him.

I grabbed the door knob, and swung the door open. The sight that greeted me caused my hand to fly in front of my mouth in horror. I grabbed the door frame to stop myself falling as I observed Oscar laying naked, on his back, on the desk, semen spurting out of his cock, which Darius had his hand wrapped around, while he fucked Oscar up the arse.

They both froze as I stood in the doorway, staring at them, and unable to move my limbs. Oscar threw his arm over his face like a child who thinks that if they can't see you, you can't see them. Darius scrambled to pull his pyjama bottoms up, and just stared at me, an unreadable emotion on his face. I turned tail and strode away. I heard Darius tell Oscar that he'd better go after me.

Back in Oscar's bedroom, I found my bag in Oscar's wardrobe and began to throw my clothes in. Oscar walked in looking dazed. "What are you doing?" he asked.

"Leaving. What does it look like?" I replied, not meeting his eyes. I couldn't bear to look at him after such a betrayal. Only two hours earlier he had declared he was in love with me, and then rushed off for a homosexual tryst. It made me feel sick.

"Elle, it's one in the morning, and we're in the middle of nowhere. Come back to bed, and we'll talk in the morning."

"Are you nuts?" I spat, "there's no way on god's green earth I'm sharing a bed with you ever again, and I'm not staying here, there's no point."

"Elle, please, be reasonable," he said, in a pleading voice.

"You're homosexual? What was I? Your beard? Your fag bangle? The cover story for your mother?" I began to recover from the initial shock, and my anger was growing.

"I'm not homosexual," he bleated, "it's only Darius, no other man. We've done it since we were kids."

"Why? Wasn't I enough for you?"

"I don't know why, we both just feel the need every now and then, and of course you're enough for me. It's a totally different thing. You and I make love. Darius and I just blow off some steam."

"Does Arabella know?"

"No. Nobody else knows. It would ruin us both if it got out. Elle, please, it's not important, you're what's important to me."

"How can you possibly say that? You just got fucked by a bloke. Do you seriously expect me to forgive and forget? It disgusts me. You used me to cover up the fact that you're gay, and I ain't playing your game." I moved to the drawer and began shoving my things into the weekend bag. I just wanted to escape, cry, and go home.

"Name your price," he said suddenly. I spun round.

"My price for what?"

"To keep this secret, this can't get out. Tell me how much you want."

I stared at him, incredulous, "I'm a fucking lawyer gayboy, I'm not gonna start blackmailing you. Keep your money, and spend it on the poor sap you end up with, cos it won't be me." I drew myself up to full height, looked him in the eye, and said; "the price of my silence is yours. Unless we are in a professional setting, you don't speak to me, look at me, or contact me. If we are at work, you will be polite. You are gonna open those gates and let me go home, and I will never breathe a word of this to a living soul. Deal'?"

He stared at me, tears forming in his eyes, "you really weren't with me for my money were you?"

"No Oscar, I wasn't. Not interested in your silly title either. Sorry to blow apart your misconceptions of the working classes," I said spitefully as I pulled on my jeans.

"A woman who was with me for all the right reasons," he said. A tear made its way out of his eye and travelled down his face. I ignored him, and pulled a jumper over my head. I zipped up my bag and grabbed my handbag.

"Open the gates for me please," was the last thing I said before I left the room. He followed me down the stairs.

"Elle, please don't go, please stay and talk about this," he pleaded. I ignored him. I had the overwhelming need to get away from him, and everything he stood for. "Elle, I love you, you know that."

I reached the large front door, unbolted it, and stomped down the steps to the drive. "At least borrow my car," Oscar said. I spun around.

"I can't drive, don't you know anything about me? No you don't, because you are so self absorbed thinking you were catch of the century that you forgot that real people have alternatives. I don't need anything from you Oscar, goodbye." I strode down the drive, not looking back. He didn't follow me.

Chapter 15

I swiped my tears away, angry at myself, at Oscar, and at Darius. I walked for about fifteen minutes at a fast pace before I reached the open gates. Then I was back in the world.

It had all felt like a bad dream, and I half expected to wake up any moment in Oscar's large bed, with him snugged into my side, warm and sleepy. Instead, I was trudging through deepest Sussex at half one in the morning. I wished James wasn't in America, I wanted to hear his voice. He would have been able to google-find a taxi. I pulled my mobile out of my handbag, it only had a bit of charge left in it. I contemplated calling my mum, but quickly dismissed the idea, knowing that she wouldn't know what to do, and it would only drain my phone.

I had no idea how to get to the nearest town, so I carried on walking down the country lane, trying to use the GPS on my phone to pull up a map. Even then, it wasn't helpful. There didn't appear to be any towns in the vicinity. In desperation, I called Roger. Thankfully he answered within three rings, and I explained that I didn't know where I was, but had left Conniscliffe and turned right. I probably sounded as panicky as I felt.

"I'll track your mobile and pinpoint you. Won't be long, just stay where you are," he said reassuringly. I stopped walking, and sat down on top of my weekend bag at the side of the road to wait, replaying the scene I'd walked in on, over and over in my head.

I'd had no inkling of Oscar and Darius' homosexuality, there had been nothing suspicious, and if Darius' wife didn't know, they must have been discreet all these years. I sucked in a deep, cleansing breath of cool night air, and shivered slightly. I had left my jacket behind at the castle, and was only wearing a thin jumper. I thanked my lucky stars for being given a driver, as in an hour or so's time, I would be back in my flat, in my own bed, and I could lick my wounds and recover from the disappointment. I sat there for about twenty minutes, listening to the night sounds of the countryside. An owl hooted, and unnamed animals rustled through the undergrowth at the side of the road.

Eventually, I heard a car approach. I kept my phone in my hand, just in case it wasn't Roger, but relaxed when I saw it was the Mercedes. It pulled up alongside me, and the window slid down.

"Are you alright?" said a Russian voice, as I stared into a pair of piercing sapphire eyes.

"Ivan? What are you doing here? I thought Roger was coming to get me," I said, embarrassed that Ivan had arrived instead. I had hoped he wouldn't find out about me phoning his driver in desperation.

"He told my bodyguard that you called, and he needed a GPS pinpoint, so I decided to come and get you, and reassure myself that you were in one piece. Jump in." I threw my bag on the back seat, and got in the passenger side. Ivan pulled away. "What did Oscar do to make you walk out in the middle of the night?"

"Nothing that I wish to divulge. Suffice to say I won't be seeing, or speaking to Oscar, or his friends, ever again."

Ivan paused, before replying;"I knew something would happen. He lives in a different world from the rest of us, with different rules. You are far too good for him."

We drove along in silence, before I spoke, "they weren't horrible to me, well his mother was at first, but we got over that. I just really want to go home, and forget about it all. I can get a taxi if you know a cab firm round here."

"Elle, it's nearly two in the morning, stay at mine tonight, I promise you'll be safe. You can meet my girls, sleep it off, and if you want to go home in the morning, Roger will take you. Women shouldn't travel alone in taxis at night, it's not safe." *Meet my girls? Wtf?*

I stayed silent. I was going to be staying at his house next week anyway, so it was no big deal to sleep there that night. I was intrigued as to who his girls, plural, were, so decided to go with the flow. I reasoned that he had come to my rescue, so it wouldn't be fair to get shirty with him. I relaxed, and watched him drive confidently and smoothly through the narrow lanes.

Eventually we stopped in front of a pair of large, wooden gates. He picked up a remote control from the dashboard, and pressed a button. The gates swung open, and we headed onwards. After a few minutes Ivan's mansion came into view, lit up by designer up lighters, it could have been described as a McMansion by a more envious individual. I thought it was beautiful. It was modern, new, but in the style of a Georgian country house. I loved it.

He stopped the car by the front door, and I got out. He grabbed my bag from the back seat, and we headed in. As soon as his key turned in the front door, I became aware of the yapping. We were greeted by two spaniels, one looking like a miniature red setter, the other, white and brown. They had the prettiest faces, and big brown eyes.

"These are my girls, the red one is Bella, the Blenheim, Tania. Do you like dogs?" Both dogs were clearly ecstatic over Ivan's return, and greeted him with enthusiastic licks.

"I love dogs. What breed are they?" I said, wondering if this was what he meant by his girls.

"Cavalier King Charles spaniels. The laziest, jolliest girls I ever met," he said, as he rubbed their ears affectionately, "alright girls, I'm home now, go find your toys." The two dogs came over to me, sniffed my hand, and raced off, presumably in search of their playthings.

I was quite surprised by the dogs. Ivan hadn't struck me as a homely type of person, let alone an animal lover. "Who looks after them when you're in London?" I asked.

"They come with me. I have a housekeeper in each place who babysits when I'm working," he replied, smiling as they returned bearing squeaky bones. "Would you like a drink?"

"I would love a cup of tea please," I said. I had never got that glass of water back at the castle, and I needed something hot and comforting. He took me through to a vast, surprisingly conservatively decorated kitchen, and filled the kettle. I looked around as I perched on a stool at the island unit to wait for my tea. The kitchen was made of wood, painted white, with granite work tops and carved edging. A squashy sofa sat at one end, and a pale wood table and chairs was placed at the other. It was a curious mixture of homely and expensive, like something a nouveau riche, Chigwell housewife would choose.

Ivan placed two steaming mugs of tea on the island, and sat down opposite me. "You look like you just got out of bed," he said, throwing a pointed look at my wild hair.

"That's because I have. I was fast asleep about two hours ago. I'm really sorry about disturbing your Saturday night, I didn't think Roger would tell you." I stared into my tea, embarrassed about needing to be rescued.

"What exactly would you have done if I hadn't been around?"

"I don't know, walked probably, or called my flatmate in the states to see if he could google a cab."

"In Sussex in the middle of the night?"

"Well, I don't know. I'm a city girl. I'm not used to there being no street names, and no passing taxis. I would have carried on walking northeast until I got to civilisation." I began to get annoyed. I had already had one argument that night, and I really didn't want another. "I can call a cab now if you would prefer me to go," I snapped.

"Don't be silly. Mrs Ballard, my housekeeper, already has the guest room ready for you, and your clothes are hung up. Roger's busy driving my date home, so I'm afraid I don't even have a spare chauffeur to lend you."

"You were on a date? I'm so sorry for interrupting you." I was mortified. Ivan saw me blush.

"Nobody of consequence. If I'm truthful, I was pleased to have an excuse to shake her off. Now, shall I show you to your room? You look exhausted." He stood up, and placed our cups in the sink. I followed him upstairs, which was formed around a gallery overlooking the entrance hall. He stopped at a door, pushed it open, and gestured for me to go in.

The room was lovely. A large bed was placed centrally against the far wall, with cream coverings, and a deeper cream headboard. The furnishings would be described as modern traditional, made of pale oak, and consisted of fitted drawers and some shelves with candles and vases on them. Ivan pointed to two doors and explained that one was the bathroom, the other, the dressing room.

He stood rather awkwardly in the room, "do you think you will make it up with Oscar?"

"No. Definitely not." I said. I half expected him to make a move on me. Instead, he just nodded and bade me goodnight as he walked out of the room.

I shed my clothes, and turned out the light before crawling into the large, soft bed. That was when it hit me that I had actually left Oscar, failed at our relationship to the point of him cheating with someone else, and had been mocked for being common. The floodgates opened, and all the fear, humiliation and regret came out in a large sob. Once it was out, I couldn't stop the tears streaming down my face. I lay in the dark, feeling sorry for myself as teardrops pooled in my ears. I vaguely heard a scratching sound at the door, then felt the bed dip slightly. A soft, warm little tongue lapped the tears off my face, while another licked my hand. As I finally drifted off, I was aware of two little bodies pressing tightly against me, the doggy equivalent of holding me tight.

I was woken the next morning by Ivan bringing me a cup of tea. He walked in with his hand shielding his eyes until he ascertained that I was decent. As I woke up, two pairs of chocolate button eyes blinked sleepily at me. Ivan laughed as Tania burrowed back into the bedclothes, covering her eyes with her paw.

"Come on lazy girls, we are wasting the day," he announced. Bella just yawned and stretched, before bouncing over the bed to say good morning to Ivan.

"What time is it?" I asked, wondering if I could snuggle in and go back to sleep.

"Nine o'clock, way past their breakfast time." Both dogs immediately pricked up their ears. "I made us bacon sandwiches, so come straight downstairs." He left me to it, and went back to the kitchen, closely followed by the two dogs. I pulled on my jeans and top from the previous night, and headed down.

The smell of bacon made my mouth water. I was ravenous, probably due to all the walking I'd done. Ivan had placed a plate of sandwiches, and a latte on the table, and was cutting up sausages for the dogs while eating his butty.

"Morning Elle, feel better?" Ivan enquired as he blew on a piece of sausage to cool it, before feeding it to a hungry looking Bella.

"Yes thanks. I'm starving though. Did you make this?" I said, indicating the plate of neatly cut sandwiches, containing perfectly crisp bacon.

"Of course. No staff except security and driver at the weekend. I like to be able to relax at home. Sunday is reserved for my girls. We eat, walk, watch telly, and sleep." He blew on another piece of sausage, this time for Tania. She practically inhaled it. "Chew darling," he admonished. She wagged her tail, and gazed up at him expectantly, willing him to give her another piece of sausage.

"Sounds lovely. I'll have a quick shower and get out of your way." I said, fascinated by his interaction with the dogs.

"Why don't you stay and join us today? You'd have to come back tonight anyway to be ready for the morning. I can show you the facilities you can use next week, and the girls can show you round the woods." He cut off another two pieces of sausage, much to the delight of the two spaniels.

"Actually, that would be lovely," I said. A walk in the woods, followed by some TV and some relaxation sounded wonderful, and after the tension of the last few days, was probably just what I needed.

We finished our breakfast, slipping stray bacon to the ever hopeful mouths below the table, and I went back to the room to shower and change. It promised to be a gloriously hot day, so I threw on a pair of shorts, and a tight T-shirt, before heading back downstairs to the kitchen.

Ivan looked astonishing in just shorts and a sleeveless, white T-shirt. He was slightly shorter than Oscar, but more muscular and defined. His legs were powerful, with large thighs and bulging calves. His shoulders and arms looked like they belonged in a diet coke break advert. In a suit, he was hot, in casual, he was a vision.

He grabbed his phone, a key, and some dog treats, and we headed out of the back door. His garden was all perfectly designed around a large outdoor pool, and pool house. Skirting around it, we headed through a rose arch, and into the woods, the girls skipping happily ahead. We walked in silence for a while, and I felt my hands unclench, and my shoulders drop as I wandered through the dappled sunshine under the canopy of trees, smelling the forest scents, and listening to the birds singing.

"It does that to everybody," Ivan said suddenly, "it makes people relax. Being close to nature has that effect. I can see the tension you're carrying disappear."

"Am I that easy to read?" I laughed.

"You were last night. You're not normally."

"So you expected me to call for international rescue this weekend then? Have you had to scoop up other girls spat out of Conniscliffe before?" This time Ivan laughed.

"No. I've never really known any of Oscar's girlfriends before, but yes, I expected you to need assistance. As I said last week, he's a complicated man with a lot of issues, one of them being his inability to relate to normal women. He either sees them as brood mares or toys for his pleasure, with nothing in between."

I pondered his words, "I guess our public school system has a lot to answer for."

"It does seem to produce a lot of screwed up men, with odd ideas," he agreed, "Russian men aren't known for their enlightened attitudes to the fairer sex, but I feel positively feminist around Oscar."

"Were you educated here or in Moscow?"

"Neither really. I was taught to read and write in Moscow, but that was about it. I came to the UK when I was fifteen, and educated myself. I read a lot."

"Why did you end up here?"

"I had to escape. The streets of Moscow are harsh when you're poor. My parents 'disappeared'," he made air quotes, "and I stowed away on trains and trucks till I got to the UK, where I claimed political asylum."

"Did you ever find out what happened to your parents?"

He paused, "yes, they were shot for being political agitators. Seventeen years ago, these things were still happening. Perestroika wasn't all rainbows and roses, as it was portrayed. I was lucky, I escaped." We walked in silence, watching the spaniels sniffing trees, and romping in the undergrowth. They seemed to have an endless capacity for fun, racing around each other in a game of tag.

"So you came and conquered London?"

Ivan smiled, "I suppose so. There's still a lot I'd like to conquer, although I could own the world, and still want the moon. It's like a sickness that I have. Do you regret losing Oscar? He would have been able to give you an amazing lifestyle."

I shook my head. "No. I have a great lifestyle as it is. I don't need to marry a man to be secure. Apart from a couple of meals out, and a bunch of flowers, I didn't have anything from Oscar. It would make me feel like a charity case to have gifts showered on me, or worse, a bought woman. Nope, not my style."

"He never took you shopping?" Ivan looked shocked. I shook my head.

"No, never. Why would he do that?"

"Every woman I ever met has demanded I take her shopping. I thought that's what women did. Considering Oscar has almost unlimited money, I would have thought a new wardrobe of clothes at the very least."

"You date the wrong women," I teased, "I didn't 'demand' anything, and I have no idea how much money Oscar has, it's none of my business."

"He has billions," said Ivan, "banking is the biggest scam in the world. They create money out of thin air, through fractional reserve banking, and get paid back real money, with interest. Nice little closed cartel too."

"It doesn't matter now," I said. "He can spend it on someone else."

"What did he do to you?" Ivan asked gently.

"Nothing I'm going to share with you. Oscar and I have a deal. I stay silent, and he stays away from me. That suits us both just fine. Can we change the subject now?"

He nodded. "Sure." Thankfully the girls came racing back, both stinking of fox poo, thoroughly pleased with themselves. "Looks like we're bathing spaniels this afternoon. Girls, you both stink," he said. I giggled.

Back at the house, Ivan disappeared to run a bath, and I plugged my dead iPhone in to charge, before helping bath two

144

wriggly, overexcited little dogs. Ivan lathered, and I rinsed, while the two dogs delighted in shaking the water out, soaking us both. By the time we'd finished, the bathroom looked like a bomb site, Ivan's hair was drenched, and my wet T-shirt had gone see through. We slid around on the wet floor, trying to each catch a spaniel to dry them off with towels, and ended up in a heap, laughing our heads off. The wet spaniels just sat wagging wet tails, spraying us both.

"That wasn't a raging success," laughed Ivan, helping me up, "you are the naughtiest girls, so don't look so pleased with yourselves." The spaniels just wagged even more.

I caught Ivan staring at my wet T-shirt, so quickly nipped back to my room to change into dry clothes. I went back downstairs to find Ivan preparing some lunch. His housekeeper had left a cold roast chicken in the fridge, and he had a pan of jersey royals boiling on the hob.

"Chicken, new potatoes and baby corn ok with you?"

"Sounds great. Anything you need me to do?"

"No, just sit and drink your wine." He pushed a glass towards me. I picked up my phone, and switched it on. There was a text from James asking if I was ok, and one from my mum, just saying hi. I quickly replied to both.

"Did Oscar check you were safe?"

"No. One from my flatmate, and one from my mum." In truth, I was a little hurt that Oscar hadn't cared about my safety. I could have been lying in a ditch for all he knew.

Chapter 16

We spent an extremely lazy and enjoyable afternoon flopping on the sofa, watching a film, with the spaniels positioned in between us, out cold, and snoring.

"One little walk, and they're worn out for the day. Lazy little things," laughed Ivan, stroking Bella's rather round, little tummy.

"They've had a busy day, walking, being bathed, eating. It's a lot for a small person." I said, before Tania let out a loud snore. We both laughed.

I discovered that Ivan was a big fan of chocolate, and we scoffed matchmakers and celebrations as we watched 'The Prince of Persia'. I loved the fact that he didn't insist on poncey chocolate, as I preferred the normal stuff. It was yet another affirmation of his lack of snobbery, which I thought was really attractive. I would never have expected 'The Russian' to have been the type to spend a day tenderly looking after dogs, and eating supermarket chocolate while sprawled out watching TV. In my mind, I'd expected him to be uptight, hyper disciplined, and a workaholic. He hadn't even had a single phone call all day, let alone done any work.

Halfway through the film, I became aware of a third snore adding to the cacophony of the dogs. I glanced over to see Ivan had fallen asleep. I stared at him, wondering if I would ever get used to how beautiful his face looked. He looked serene and boyish, at odds with his powerful, intensely masculine body. Ignoring the film, I replayed our day together in my mind. For two people who didn't know each other well, we had been remarkably relaxed in each other's company, rather like the easy relationship I had with James. I had to remind myself that he was a sharp talking billionaire who I'd witnessed sharking a client. I mentally slapped

146

myself for thinking how nice and normal he was, when in reality he was beautiful beyond belief, and as sharp as a knife. I steeled myself against being seduced. In the meantime, I could enjoy the pretty... Ok, I was being a bit creepy with the 'staring while he's asleep' thing, but if I was being honest, I wanted to get over his looks, and stop them affecting me, although I was puzzled as to why he hadn't made a move on me. If he did, I wasn't entirely sure I'd want to resist.

Eventually, Bella nuzzled him awake, and he scrubbed at his face, before checking his watch. "Ok baby girl, yes I know, it's tea time." He wandered out to the kitchen with the dogs at his heels, and reappeared a few minutes later bearing glasses of wine. The film had long finished, and I was watching a crappy game show. "Shall I show you round the house?"

I followed him down a corridor, and into his home gym. It was really well equipped, and with the pool, had everything I'd need. We carried on to the library, which was beautiful. Ivan took a piece of paper, and wrote down his wifi password for me, so I could use the Internet on my laptop.

"I'd rather you didn't use my study, if that's ok," he said. I nodded. *What secrets have you got then Ivan?*

He showed me how to summon security, and how to use his panic room, which was extremely well fitted out with food, water and communications. "Why all the security?" I asked.

"I made a lot of enemies over the years," was his flippant reply, "quite a few would love a pop at me, so I make sure I'm well protected."

We decided on a swim before dinner. I changed into my costume, and wrapped a towel round myself. Ivan was already swimming when I got there. I climbed in, and began a front crawl, which soon turned into a race. Ivan was a good swimmer, but I was faster. We did length after length as he tried to catch me up, never quite managing it, but the chase itself was exhilarating,

Eventually, I stopped at the edge of the pool, and waited as Ivan caught up. We were both panting and breathless from the exertion. "Are you some kind of Olympic swimmer?" Ivan asked, between trying to catch his breath.

I grinned, "no, but I do swim every day." I glided away from him, and lay floating on my back, looking up at the sky. A pair of hands shoved me from underneath, launching me into the air, before I landed back in the water with a splash. Ivan popped up from under the surface, and began to laugh at me spluttering.

"That's not fair," I yelled, before diving under the water, and grabbing his feet, causing him to flail his arms wildly to keep himself from sinking.

I let go of his feet, and came up for air, smoothing my wet hair back off my face. Ivan was staring at me. "You are so beautiful Elle, you know that don't you?"

"That's really sweet of you to say, Ivan, thank you," I replied, "and you are very handsome too."

"But?"

"But nothing. You're handsome." I smiled, and swam away from him to get out of the pool. The early evening air was cool, and made me shiver slightly. To my absolute horror, my nipples hardened into bullets. I grabbed the towel and wrapped it round me, fully aware that Ivan had gotten an eyeful, as I could see lust written all over his face. For a split second, I let myself imagine what it would be like to have those lust filled sapphire eyes staring into mine, as he made wild, passionate love to me. I shoved that thought out of my head, and asked him if he was getting out.

"Give me a few minutes, and I'll be out," he said, looking uncomfortable.

"Ok, no problem," I said, turning to walk back to the house, and give him some privacy. Inwardly, I was high fiving myself. I jumped in the shower to wash the chlorine off, and then pulled on my pyjamas and robe. Back downstairs, I poured another glass of wine each, and settled down on the sofa for Sunday night telly. Ivan took ages in the shower, eventually appearing halfway through Top Gear. He flopped down on the sofa, and gave Tania's ears an affectionate rub, before grabbing his wine, and taking a big slug.

"What time are you leaving in the morning? I asked.

"About seven." I felt quite bereft at the thought of not seeing him again until Friday, but given the task I had to complete in the next week, it was probably a good thing not to be distracted. If he had been at home, I would have had to stay at the Travelodge so as not to be tempted.

"Are you hungry?" He asked.

"Not really, but I could eat if you are." He jumped up, and disappeared into the kitchen. About ten minutes later, he came back carrying a tray laden with snacks. Between the four of us, we managed to demolish the contents fairly quickly. The girls getting more than their fair share. It was all very cosy and domestic, and it made me miss James, and the easy familiarity we shared.

By ten I was yawning, so said my good nights, and headed up to bed. Ivan took the girls outside for their final wee, and I heard him talking to them as the three of them headed to his bedroom. I lay in the darkness, trying not to think of him laying, possibly naked, just across the hall. Was he laying awake thinking about me? Or was he thinking about the date he sent home on Saturday night? I allowed myself to fantasise about him coming to my bedroom, declaring that he just had to have me. I knew he would never behave like that, but I still held my breath as I heard the bedroom door creak open.

I felt the bed dip slightly, and a cold, wet nose nuzzled my hand. I couldn't see which one it was, so I just gave her ears a little rub, and listened to her snuffly breathing as I fell asleep.

As per usual, I was up bright and early. I discovered that Tania had spent the night with me, and looked as though she had no intention of getting up early. After pulling on shorts and a T-shirt, I ventured down to the kitchen to make tea. Sitting on the patio, sipping my cuppa, I focused my mind on the day ahead. I decided not to tackle Mrs Smith about her less than complimentary description of me to Lady Golding, as I figured that we had enough rope to sack her at the disciplinary hearing we had planned, failing that, I knew that we could make her position so difficult, she'd beg to retire. I drained my cup, and headed into the gym, and straight onto the treadmill. I needed to clear the cobwebs of the difficult weekend away, and work off some of the food I'd eaten. I could hear Ivan talking to the dogs in the kitchen as I used the weights machine.

I did my workout, headed out to the pool, and was just finishing my swim, when Ivan appeared, dressed in a navy suit and crisp, white shirt. He was fresh from the shower, and his hair was still damp, and slightly tousled.

"Just off. Thought I'd come and say goodbye."

"Have a good week, and I'll probably see you Friday, although I'm sure I'll speak to you before that," I said, switching into professional mode, which was tricky when I was just wearing a swimsuit. Ivan just stood there, as if he wanted to say something, he frowned slightly.

"Er yes, ok, Friday. Be good." He turned tail and left. I finished my swim, and dried off, before going back into the kitchen. A small, dark haired woman was wiping down the surfaces.

"Hello, you must be Ms Reynolds," she said pleasantly, "I'm Ivan's housekeeper, Mrs Ballard, but please call me Jo."

"Nice to meet you, please call me Elle. Has Ivan gone?"

"Yes, about ten minutes ago. Now, what would you like for breakfast?"

"Some toast and a latte would be great thanks, but I can make it, I don't want to put you out."

"Not at all, it's lovely to have someone here during the week. I mostly just clean the house, and get it ready for the weekend, so it's nice to actually do some cooking for someone. Ivan tells me you're working at the big factory near Derwent all week?"

I sat down on a stool, "yep, sorting out their antiquated systems. No doubt I'll be dusty and cross by tonight."

"My brother works there. He is delighted that it's finally being sorted. He was always paid by cheque, usually wrong or late, then had to wait five days for it to clear, so anything will be an improvement." She placed a coffee in front of me, and began buttering my toast.

"Funny enough, none of the employees have been difficult about it, apart from the old lady who currently runs personnel, she hates my guts, although, to be fair, I did shout at her and make her cry."

"Marion Smith? Hmm, maybe you should have a look at what she's been hiding," said Jo, rather cryptically, "she had an affair with the managing director years ago, and has always been strangely untouchable despite being rubbish at her job. All the employees have complained about her, and nothing ever got done about it." *Interesting..*

"I'll keep my eyes open," I said, before starting on my toast. Jo changed the subject, asking me my food preferences, as she would be preparing my meals all week.

It was nice to chat to someone normal, who wasn't wealthy, posh, or beautiful. While I sipped my coffee, she told me about her husband, and two grown up children, and I felt a pang of homesickness for the normality of a working class life. Rather reluctantly, I made my way upstairs to shower, and prepare myself for the day ahead. Roger was picking me up at half eight for the ten minute journey to the factory. It all felt very leisurely and relaxed compared to a normal Monday morning.

Roger was in a good mood, greeting me with a cheery 'good morning', and humming along to the radio. I asked him about Saturday night, and he rather evasively answered that 'Mr Porenski sent me on an errand to Surrey'. I didn't question further, not wanting to embarrass him, or put him in an awkward position. We pulled into the car park, and I steeled myself for the day that lay ahead. Just to add to the madness, new filing cabinets were being delivered that day, so that when we were done, the paper files could be stored properly, and neatly, rather than on the rickety shelves. It was going to be a testing day.

My trainees were all in and at their desks by ten to nine, bright eyed and bushy tailed. Their cases stored ready for the minibus to the hotel that evening. As the first employees came filing in, we scrambled to find their paper files, and deliver them to the correct people to begin the arduous process all over again. Mrs Smith eventually showed up at twenty five past nine, huffing that the traffic had been bad. "In Sussex? Traffic?" Was all I replied. She seemed nervous and edgy around me, but we were too busy for me to take much notice of her. The disciplinary meeting was scheduled for Friday afternoon, when, hopefully we would be finished processing the employees.

Laura had emptied all the boxes of loose papers, sorted the ones that had to be added to employee files, and put the remainder in alphabetical order. It cleared space for the new filing cabinets, which arrived at eleven.

With Marion finding files as we needed them, I was free to input the data we missed on Friday. All the employees we had already processed turned up with their ID and bank details, as requested, and I was able to close the files on them. I called Lewis to assure him everything was going well, that we would be done by Friday, ahead of schedule, and asked him to approve two weeks off at the end of July.

"Knew you'd be fine," he said, "I'll check on those holiday dates, but I can't see why not. I'll call you back in an hour." I got back to work, inputting the salary details from the vast ledgers into the employee files on the computer. It was arduous and painfully slow work. The manager had placed a pencil line through every employee already entered, so I did the same. He was dealing with suppliers all day, so had escaped the presence of the irritating and bumbling Mrs Smith. I had to stop myself being snarky with her over her constant whining about being tired, too hot and her bad back. If she said that the new system wouldn't work one more time, I would have to nail my hand to the desk to stop myself slapping her.

At quarter to twelve, she picked up her bag, and announced that she was going to lunch. I was about to challenge her, when Lewis called to tell me the dates I'd requested for my holiday had been approved. By the time I'd finished on the phone, the old cow had disappeared. I noted the times and dates down in my iPhone as further ammunition to oust her on Friday. I also text James to tell him I'd booked two weeks off, and ask how his new job was going.

Just as I put my phone back down on the desk, Roger popped his head round the door, "Lady Golding is here to see you. She requested to speak to you in private, is that ok?"

I groaned, "yes, would you mind showing her into room 16 please?" *What the hell did that old bag want?* I picked up my phone and handbag, and trotted down the corridor to the spare office. Bracing myself, I strode in confidently, my impassive, professional, don't-mess-with-me face on. She stood when I walked in. I shook her rather limp hand. She looked nervous.

"Lady Golding, how nice to see you, I wasn't expecting you. Please take a seat. Can I offer you a tea or coffee?" She sat down in front of the desk. I sat behind it.

"Tea would be nice, thank you," she replied. I stuck my head out of the door, and asked Laura, who was passing, to bring two teas. "I came to see if you were alright," she said, uncertainty clouding her features, "and to thank you for your help on Saturday morning."

There was a thick silence until Laura arrived with our drinks, setting them down on the desk, and disappearing quickly. "Why don't you tell me the real reason you're here?" I said, taking a sip. She looked uncomfortable, and shifted in her chair.

"Oscar told me what happened. He's in a terrible state over you. I've never seen him like this, and I don't really know what to do. I'm so worried that he'll go back to his old ways." Her words came out in a rush, and in a moment of clarity, I saw that she was just a mother worried for her son, and not the mean, vicious old harridan I'd assumed she was at first meeting. She fished around in her bag for a hanky, and dabbed her eyes.

"I doubt very much that he told you the truth of what happened. I'm certainly not going to tell you. I'm sure Oscar will be over me, and onto the next girl fairly quickly," I said, wanting to shut the conversation down.

"He told me you caught him with Darius, in an unmentionable act," she said. My mouth dropped open. "Then he said he offered you money to stay quiet about it, but that you were disgusted that he thought you would blackmail him, that if he left you alone, you would never speak of it. Is all of that the truth?"

"Why did he tell you?" I still didn't want to confirm or deny anything. Lawyer training kicked in. She looked sheepish.

"He told me because when I discovered you'd walked out in the middle of the night, I wrongly made the assumption that it had been your fault, and I wasn't very complimentary. He also told me it was you that Mrs Smith had been spouting off about, which of course, I'd repeated at dinner."

"You weren't to know who that toxic old bat was talking about," I muttered.

"I know, it doesn't excuse my rudeness though, especially as you were so helpful getting it so beautifully done."

I shrugged. "I don't know what you expect me to say or do, Lady Golding. I'm sorry Oscar regrets what he did, but I did nothing wrong, and he needs to accept that I'm no longer in his life. He's far better suited to a less, how shall I put it, ordinary girl than me, and I'm sure he'll find a nice titled lady settle down with, and you'll all be pleased I'm out of the picture."

"You're far from ordinary Elle, you could have asked him for millions, yet you acted with total integrity. He realises what he's lost, and he's beside himself with regret."

"As I explained to Oscar, I'm a lawyer. My career is more important than a few million, which I can earn legitimately for myself. Blackmailing someone would get me struck off, and I fought way too hard to get here, to just throw it away for someone else's mistake. Now, perhaps if Oscar had been turned down a few more times in his life, he would have been better equipped to deal with this, but we all have disappointments to deal with at times. I didn't have much fun trudging through country lanes, lost, cold, and upset on Saturday night, but I got over it."

"How on earth did you get home?"

"I called my driver as soon as I realised there was no village nearby, and he used GPS to pinpoint my mobile phone, and come and rescue me." I didn't need to tell her about Ivan. "I'm a city girl, with no experience of the country. I had no idea how to get back to London. Oscar knew that, and still let me walk out alone. A gentlemen would never have behaved like that."

"You have no idea how appalled I am at his behaviour, Elle, all of it. I wish none of it had happened, but he's still my son, and I hate seeing him in so much pain."

"So did you come here to try and persuade me to go back to him?"

"I'm not sure. I wanted to apologise to you, and see if there was a possibility you could forgive him." She looked at me hopefully.

"I don't hate him, but I can't possibly be with him. I couldn't live with his predilection. I also found out that I couldn't live in your world, so there's nothing to forgive. My best advice is to go home, give him a cuddle, and let him be the man he wants to be, without the pressure to become what you think is right."

She stared at me, making me nervous that I'd said the wrong thing. "You really are the one that got away, no wonder he's so upset. He should have grabbed you with both hands, and never let you go while he had the chance. Now, if there's ever anything you need, please don't hesitate to come to me. I owe you a debt for your silence."

"It's not your debt, Lady Golding, but I can assure you that our secret will go to the grave with me. I have no desire to ruin Oscar, or even Darius for that matter. Now, if you'll excuse me, I have a lot of work I need to be getting on with, and an old bat to bully." I stood up, and shook her hand, before she left, escorted by Roger. A horrid thought struck me, I hoped Roger hadn't been eavesdropping on our conversation. Knowing Ivan's habit of bugging offices, I couldn't be 100% sure.

Chapter 17

Staying at the house was wonderful. Jo was extremely hospitable and efficient, providing wonderful meals, and laundering my clothes each day. The week seemed to be flying by, and we were making fantastic progress at the factory. My trainee legal staff had been working diligently and methodically, and we had made huge inroads in the ancient paper system. Even Marion had piped down, and was sulkily embracing the changes. The interim manager even commissioned a cleaning team to tackle the accumulation of dust and dirt in the offices, so it was a more pleasant environment to work in.

James text to tell me that he was enjoying California, the geeks he was in charge of we're alright, and not too greasy, and that he was delighted that I'd booked time off work, and would begin researching holidays. I missed him, and our flat, and was really looking forward to getting back on Friday, even though he wouldn't be there. Ivan's house was lovely, but I was a bit sick of all the security that watched my every movement, and felt the need for some privacy and quiet.

By midday on Friday, every member of staff had been seen, according to the foreman's lists. Strangely there were still files unclaimed, and ledger entries not accounted for. I quickly typed a list of names that hadn't been seen, and went in search of the foreman. He scanned the list, looking puzzled.

"Never heard of any of those people," he said, shaking his head.

"Not off sick, holiday, or paternity leave?" I probed.

"No. Nobody on long term sick at the moment, and certainly no pregnant men," he joked, "and we close for two week summer holiday, and two weeks at Christmas. I know every worker in this factory, and I don't know those names."

I nodded, "thanks for all your help," and went back to the office. I checked the ledgers again, getting the final pay figure for the previous month, then ran a simulation on the new system. It was over two hundred thousand pounds less. Puzzled, I looked in the company cheque books, and uncovered the scam. I called Ivan.

"I think I've uncovered an issue," I said without preamble.

"Go on," he replied.

"Right, well, the factory was paying a thousand and twenty staff each month by cheque, and on the statements, it doesn't say where the cheques went, just the numbers. We have inputted all the staff now, and we are just over a hundred short. I ran a simulation, and the wage bill will be two hundred grand less a month than before. I think there were just over a hundred ghost employees."

He whistled through his teeth, "well done Elle, that's some serious cash being sucked out each month, and nearly two and a half million a year. I suspected there may have been some, but not on that scale. I'm going to pay a visit this afternoon. Keep that personnel woman there until I get there please."

"We have her booked in for a disciplinary meeting at two. Will you make that, or should I delay it?"

"I'll be there. In the meantime, speak to Lewis about the contractual issues that this throws up with the previous owners, as there has been fraud."

He cut the call, leaving me standing with the phone in my hand. *I really must speak to him about learning to say hi and bye.*

I called Lewis, and told him what I'd found. He was shocked at the scale of the fraud, and pointed out that Ivan's bill to the firm would be repaid with just one month's savings on the payroll. He promised to scour the sale contract, and find an angle to sue for breach of contract due to payroll fraud.

I collected the paper files that related to the ghost workers, finally emptying the shelves and checked the contents of a few. Blank paper and unsigned photocopies had been stuffed in to make them look legit. I put them in a box, along with the pay ledgers, and instructed Roger to keep guard over them until Ivan arrived.

When the last of the filing had been completed, and the system checked for any missing paperwork (there wasn't any), I let all the trainees go home, thanking them for their hard work, and their attention to detail. With every employee file up to date, and linked into the clocking in system, my work was done.

Marion arrived back from lunch extremely late, just as the maintenance men were dismantling the rickety old shelves in her office. "Hey, what are they doing? Those shelves are useful storage," she complained.

"No useful storage needed now. The computer is the storage, and the shiny new filing cabinets. Now Marion, would you like to take the typewriter home so that you can continue to type out the church newsletter? Lady Golding did mention that you could only do it at work due to not possessing a typewriter at home." I smiled brightly at her look of utter horror.

"You were the one who did it instead," she said.

"Yep. Corrected all your terrible spelling too, and for your information, I am indeed Mr Porenski's lawyer, well one of them, and no I'm not sleeping with him. I like to think I can make my way in the world using my brains, not my body. You might want to tell that to Lady Golding."

She went bright red, "I can't believe she told you."

"She didn't know you were talking about me, I was there as her son's girlfriend, and I had to listen to all your opinions of me over dinner. So I suggest you think before you gossip in future. Lady Golding is terribly embarrassed that she repeated it, not knowing I was sitting at her table."

Before she had a chance to answer, the manager came in to request her presence in the disciplinary meeting. He informed me that I would be required too. We followed him down the corridor to the old chairman's office, where Ivan was already seated. He stood as we entered the room, and indicated that Marion should be seated opposite him at the large desk. I sat beside her, and the manager beside Ivan. Marion glanced nervously at Ivan's security detail who were by the door.

Ivan spoke first, "good afternoon Mrs Smith, I'm Mr Porenski, your employer. We're you made aware of your right to be accompanied today by a colleague or trades union representative?"

"Oh yes, but I don't need one. This is all just a silly misunderstanding about a newsletter and a piece of paper."

Ivan looked quizzical. "Mrs Smith, who are John Knox, David Logan, Peter Merdy, and all the other names that you have been paying cheques to for years, that don't work here?" He handed her the list. I watched carefully as she went very pale. A sheen of sweat appeared on her top lip.

"I don't know," she said, "I just did the payroll."

"You wrote out the cheques," said Ivan, "the stubs are in your handwriting. Who were you making those cheques out to?"

"I don't know what cheques you're talking about," she said, playing dumb.

Ivan's fist crashed down on the desk, making us all jump. He stood and bellowed at her, "DON'T LIE TO ME, I WILL NOT BE LIED TO, DO YOU UNDERSTAND?" He was absolutely terrifying, and I prayed I'd never be on the receiving end of his temper. Marion looked panicked, and began to shake.

Then the most awful, horrific thing happened, Marion wet herself. It ran down the chair legs and splashed loudly onto the floor. When Ivan realised what was happening, his eyes widened in shock. I actually had to move my chair out of the way to avoid a puddle of piss round my shoes. She sat in her wet skirt, covered in urine, in front of Ivan, and cried.

"It was Mr Morgan, the managing director, "she sobbed, struggling to get the words out, "he, he made me. Then when it was sold, said we should carry on, that he was getting what was rightfully his."

Ivan held his hand up for her to stop. "Mrs Smith, this is a police matter now. Your manager will call them, and give them the tape of this meeting, and they will investigate. You are dismissed from this company with immediate effect for theft, which is classed as a gross misconduct. There will be no pay in lieu of notice or severance pay, and we shall co operate with any police action brought against you. Do you understand?" She nodded weakly. "Good day to you. Elle, come with me please." Ivan rose and walked around the desk. We left Mrs Smith and the manager in there.

"Oh god, that was horrific," he said, striding down the corridor. "I can't believe that just happened. You didn't get it on your shoes did you?"

"I think I got out of the firing line just in time."

"Good, now I need to get back to London. Join me in my car." *Please would be nice.*

"Roger has my bags."

"I had them moved to my car. Lets go." His security held open the rear doors of a large, silver Bentley. We got in, and a bodyguard got in the front seat next to the driver. Once we'd moved off, Ivan pressed a button to lift the privacy screen. He opened the bar to pull out a bottle of Krug, deftly opening it in the confined space. He handed me a glass. "To a profitable partnership."

I clinked his glass, "cheers."

Krug on an empty stomach is not a great idea. After just one glass, I began to feel light headed. Ivan's close proximity and delicious scent began to affect me. I took a bottle of water from my handbag, and glugged it down. It was warm, and a bit stale, but did the job. My head cleared a little.

"How long are you going to deny your attraction to me?" Ivan asked, putting me on the spot.

"I don't deny that you're very attractive Ivan, but I'm not going to throw myself at you."

"I see, why's that?"

"One, I work for you, indirectly I know, but still. Two, I just got away from Oscar, and three, you only date models."

"Do I get the opportunity to answer those concerns?"

"Be my guest." *This was getting exciting.*

"One, you work for Pearson Hardwick, not me. I would employ you in a flash, but doubt that I could lure you away, or compete with the other big law firms for your employment. Two, you don't seem heartbroken over Oscar. I know you cried on Saturday night, but after that, you were fine, that tells me you weren't in love with him, and three, you are far prettier and more intriguing than any model I ever met. Does that answer you?"

"You scare me," I admitted. "Does that surprise you?"

160

He looked shocked. "How do I scare you? You saw me with the girls, how soft I am."

"I also just saw you make an old lady piss herself in fear. I watched you try and scam a client. Yes you're lovely with the dogs, but it doesn't take away from the fact that you're an alpha male. You even approach this like a business transaction. I place my objections, you counter, and a shag is pencilled into our schedules. It's not how I conduct my relationships."

"So tell me, what do I need to do?"

"Ivan, I'm not going to do that. If its meant to be, it'll happen. I'm not giving you a tick list. If your approach is a turn off for me, I don't expect you to change."

He grabbed my hand, and held it to his perfect lips, "you see, Elle, I think you and I would have the hottest, rawest sex together. I think I could make you come so hard that you forget your own name." *Jesus Christ, that is definitely a voice made for phone sex.* Everything south of my waist tightened. *No hearts or flowers though, just a sexual plaything to a rich man.* I snatched my hand away.

"I don't want what you're offering Ivan. Sorry."

"Oh Elle, you're a hard woman."

I stared out of the window silently for the rest of the drive while Ivan caught up on phone calls, jabbering in Russian in most of them. I asked the driver to stop at a garage, so I could pick up some necessities, and before I knew it, we were pulling up outside my flat.

"Thanks for the lift," I said, clambering out of the car. The driver opened the boot, and pulled out my case and bag.

"Elle, thank you for uncovering all that this week. It was a great job done," said Ivan. I grabbed my bags and went home.

The first thing I did was put a coffee on, the second was to phone Lewis. "Hi, I'm back. Any developments?"

"I spoke to Porenski and advised him how to proceed. It worked in his favour because with correct payroll costs, the company is more profitable than expected. We just filed a minor damages claim for mis-representation, but beyond that, he's better keeping quiet and enjoying the extra profit."

"Do you need me to come back to work? It's only four."

"No, but I think you should meet us in Lauren's bar at five. Drinks are on me."

"That sounds great. See you in a bit."

I unpacked my bag and hung all my laundered clothes up in my dressing room, before changing into jeans and flats and heading over to the bar. All my workmates were there, enjoying bottles of cold beer at the end of a hard week. I got a cheer when I walked in, and a cold bottle of bud pressed into my hand. I took a long draught. Lewis sidled up.

"Do you want the good news? Or the really good news?"

"Go on."

"You have a meeting with Ms Pearson on Monday to discuss your salary and status. You need to go over to head office. Your meetings at ten."

"Wow! Is that the good or really good news?"

"Just the good. Wait for this, due to Mr Porenski's patronage, and the fact that he's been raving about us, well you really, we have gained five large blue chip clients this week alone, snatched from under the noses of our competitors. Worth millions a year each, with more firms expressing interest and sounding us out. How great is that? You make sure you get a decent pay rise."

I clinked bottles with Lewis. "By the way, how much should I ask for?" I whispered in his ear.

"Ask for 250k, settle on 200. Ask for a performance bonus of 100% of basic salary for every million you generate in revenue. I didn't just tell you that, capiche?" I winked at him and grinned. I truly had arrived.

End of Book One

Other books by D A Latham

The Beauty and the Blonde

ABOUT THE AUTHOR

D A Latham is a salon owner, mother of Persian cats, and devoted partner to the wonderful Allan.

16961084R00094

Printed in Great Britain
by Amazon